Dangerous Regrets

The Men of Machismo

by

Morgan Kay

Chapter One

O N A TUESDAY afternoon, the library resembled a morgue, minus the stiffs. Darcy pushed the fiction cart toward the book stacks. Her eyes flickered over the spines of the recently returned books. The usual collection of well-worn cozy mysteries and romances featured billionaires and Navy seals. The occasional author managed to combine both. Perhaps, that was her problem, no billionaires or hot military men in the stories she penned. So far, no agents begging to represent her.

The low sound of voices punctured her absorption in her non-existent writing career.

"It has to be now."

The urgency in the man's voice had her abandoning her cart. Her soft-soled shoes allowed her to move down the aisle without a squeak or a telltale footfall. It could be nothing, but it might also be a bit of conversation she could include in her next literary effort. If her granny were still alive, she'd mention *that eavesdroppers never heard anything good about themselves.*

"You owe me."

The gruff reply had her peering around shelved books to see who was talking. Monrovia wasn't exactly a huge town, so she should be able to recognize the men. The first voice sounded somewhat familiar, but she couldn't quite place it. The second one she didn't know. All that meant was he'd never be in the library, taught at the local school, or was a relation.

The first man's voice grew shriller. "I had nothing to do with you getting nabbed. You can't blame that on me."

Darcy tiptoed closer, trying to see who was speaking. An expanse of black broadcloth material came into view. She blinked. My goodness, she didn't realize how close she was. Her initial impression of the men speaking in normal voices must have been a mistake due to the absolute silence in the building.

"Don't believe it for a second. I figured you took off with the emeralds and left me pay the price for the heist you engineered."

Darcy gasped. *Emeralds.* Heist. It sounded like a movie of the week. Footsteps signaled one of the men had sidled to one side. Her position, peering through an open place on the shelf, allowed her to only see the back of one of the speakers, but she could still hear.

"No, never. I had second thoughts about the whole deal, which is the reason I changed careers."

"Ha! I know you're sitting on them until you can move them. I expect my share. The way I figure it, you owe me more for my time spent in the pen. Cross me again and you're a dead man!"

The vehemence underlying the words had her stumbling backwards and knocking a paperback thriller over.

"What was that?"

Darcy hit the floor. Her body trembled as she crawled down the aisle as if she were under fire, stirring up dust as she went. The men were still talking as opposed to hunting for her. Her breath sounded loud in her ears as she reached the end of the aisle where the summer reading program boxes provided a welcome shield.

Her small size allowed her to work her way into the center of the boxes. She grabbed one box and pulled it in place as footsteps passed her. Her heart managed to dislodge itself from its normal location and work its way up into her throat. *Thank goodness, no one saw me.*

Curiosity got the better of her, causing her to push the box aside an inch to see the black suit and the back of a balding head. Her head jerked back. She had the same view at church the previous Sunday.

A heavier footfall had her shrinking back against a box as a bald man with a mangled face that indicated a history of fighting came closer. His dark eyes stared straight at the boxes causing her to hold her breath. It felt like he could see right inside the dark cave the stacked boxes made. Thank goodness, she'd been slow to move the boxes to the basement as asked. Sweat beaded her upper lip as she peered through a crack, waiting for the man to move on. He hesitated and surveyed the area.

Baldy, as she nicknamed him in her head, turned all the way around in search of witnesses. Darcy's cheeks puffed out, and her face flushed as she struggled to hold her breath. It had never been her strong point, which is why she eeked out a C in swimming. Finally, the man moved on, allowing her to breathe again.

Would he remember her at the circulation desk? Worse, would he notice she wasn't at the desk on his way out? That wouldn't necessarily mean she'd eavesdropped on them. She could have been in the backroom or the bathroom. Technically, she'd been the only one on duty since her boss, Leticia Blankenship, took off for lunch.

Darcy waited in dark, hot space waiting for the men to leave the place. Her luminous watch face counted off five minutes, managing to stretch it into hours. Surely, enough time passed to safely exit her hiding place. She pushed the box aside and crawled out. A pair of no nonsense Oxfords met her initial glance. Her eyes continued up past the orthopedic hose and the wool pleated skirt past the peter pan blouse, to the lips pulled down in a disapproving expression. Leticia tsked as she crawled out of her cardboard sanctuary.

Darcy stood dusting off her dress to no avail. This morning she had second thoughts about the wispy white dress as work wear. She'd considered spaghetti sauce as an issue, not blood, possibly hers. The woman glared at her through her half-moon glasses. "Give her a chance, your mother pleaded. She's a great reader. Bound to be able to recommend books."

It had been no secret that Leticia Blankenship did not appreciate her creative turn of a phrase, especially when caught turning said phrase at work. The fact she had time to write demonstrated the lack of actual duties, which meant her measly job could end. All Leticia needed was someone to spot her during her lunch hour and operate the circulation counter when she held book talks. While the pay wasn't extravagant, even the laugh-worthy amount kept her in Ramen noodles and Sylvester, her kitty, in cat food. Well, this job and her second part-time job waiting tables at the local bar and grill did.

"You won't believe what happened when you were gone." She held her hands up knowing she had a legitimate reason for crawling out from the summer reading boxes cave like a toddler.

The woman crossed her arms and sniffed. "This I have to hear." She held up her index finger and wagged it. "No more of your far-fetched lies that you refer to as stories, either."

Darcy pressed her hand against her chest. How could a woman who worked in a library have such a hatred for fiction? "Two men were talking about stolen emeralds in the D-H fiction section. Our library is an assignation spot for felons. You won't believe who one of them is?"

Before she could continue, Leticia's hand flew up, palm out, in a stop fashion. "No more. I'm tired of your Elven visitors at the local tulip festival."

"Wait, he could have been an elf. Tall, slender, long blonde hair, and pointed ears."

Leticia's frown deepened. "I'm tired of this. Elves. Aliens. Now, felons planning emerald heists in our library."

Not only did the woman not welcome an observant eye and an open mind, she was a bad listener, too. "They already had the heist. They were arguing about the emeralds, and one of them was my—"

"No more. I refuse to listen to your nonsense." She pivoted on her heel and marched down the aisle.

The angular frame, the pursed mouth, the crabby attitude reminded Darcy of another literary character, Leticia wouldn't appreciate the comparison. Might as well get back to work.

She slid into her chair at the circulation desk, grateful the high desk hid most of the dirt-smeared dress, but not enough. The squeak-squeak of the shelving cart came closer, which meant Leticia would have another run at her.

The woman rounded the desk and shook her head. "Go home. You're a mess. Don't waste your time calling the county law enforcement agency. I already warned the sheriff, Donald, my cousin, you might."

Darcy reached for her purse wondering at what cost this unexpected short shift came. "I'll be back tomorrow at nine."

"Let me think about that. I'll have to consider how long your mama and I have been friends. I don't understand why you can't be more like your brother, William."

Ah yes, the golden child, William, who never did anything wrong. Despite being named Fitz William after her mother's favorite Jane Austen hero, it didn't seem to taint him the way Darcy did her. Of course, William lost the Fitz immediately since her father read somewhere it referred to illegitimacy. Her father, a man of firm opinions, didn't want anyone calling his son illegitimate.

Darcy's name, on the other hand, caused her no end of frustration, telling teachers and playmates that her first name wasn't her last name. It didn't help that the family's last name was Darlington. It made her sound as if she were part of a bizarre tongue twister.

"You're not the first person to ask me that." She shrugged, not wanting to elaborate. Most of the time, she liked her twin, William, like everyone else. The man with his helpful attitude was hard not to like. Only when people wanted to know why they were so different, implying Darcy wasn't quite right, did she resent William the tiniest little bit. It would be helpful if the man would do something reprehensible for a change and take the heat off her.

She shouldered her bag and waved goodbye to her boss. At least she hoped she was her boss and not her former one. Her rust-dotted car rested next to the curb. She'd love something newer and sportier, but that would have to wait until she became a famous author. At this rate, it wouldn't be in her lifetime.

A navy muscle car slowed as it came to a stop sign at the end of the road. It allowed Darcy a chance to check out the occupant, a man with strong features and a short haircut. Possibly a Navy Seal, a billionaire, or a billionaire former Navy Seal. Whoever he was she knew he didn't live around here.

Her second job at Sweaty's, which she thought was a terrible name for a sports bar, gave her the opportunity at one time or another to wait on the pick of the town's bachelors accompanied by their dates. It would be hard to forget that profile. The man turned and smiled at her. What had started as a mediocre day, and then took an abrupt turn south, showed signs of improvement. Her hand went up, and she waved her fingers in a flirty wave.

Ronny Benson rolled up behind the man in his jacked-up truck and slammed on his horn.

Darcy cringed at Dixie being played at ear-blasting decibels. The unknown handsome man drove away. Figures. Whenever she was within spitting distance of anything good, Fate bitch slapped her.

"Hey, sweet cheeks, wha' cha doing?" Ronny leaned out the window of this truck reminding her that she'd been so desperate she went out with him once. Even though it had been several years ago, that one date created a belief in Ronny that they had an on and off relationship. It had been off for about as long as she could remember, but Ronny remained hopeful.

"I'm leaving one job to go to another." She opened her car door, releasing a wave of heat.

Ronny stared down at her from his high perch with a wide grin. Darcy grabbed the back of her dress, pulling the bodice back to prevent the man from peeking at her breasts. The truck kept her from pulling out. Apparently, Ronny hadn't finished his run at her.

"You wouldn't have to work if you were my gal. I got a brand new double wide."

The broken driver's side window that wouldn't roll down and the sweltering interior temperature forced her to crack open the car door as she spoke. Ronny would see it as a sign that she might be caving into his dubious charms. A twist of her wrist had the engine running and in a few minutes, it would be safe to turn the air conditioner on.

"Yes, I heard all about it. Even the Jacuzzi in the master bath but I have to get to work. I'd appreciate it if you could move your truck."

He gave her a two-finger salute, but refused to take the hint. With any luck, she wouldn't see him at Sweaty's. It was even harder to give Ronny the brush-off in public. Too many people thought they were an item. She wasn't sure if it was his numerous appearances at Sweaty's when she was working or possibly the rumors he spread that they'd done the nasty. In a small town like Monrovia that equaled putting a bumper sticker across her body, declaring her property of Ronny Benson.

"Ah, you're keeping tabs on me." His eyebrows lifted as his smile stretched revealing his gold tooth.

As much as it pained her, Darcy needed an explanation for her knowledge. "Why a man like you isn't married in a town with few eligible men confounds me. People talk." She knew exactly why he wasn't married. His bullying behavior that pinned her into her parking place said it all. If she wanted to leave before Christmas, then that meant applying a little sugar. Her father grumbled she hadn't learn anything at college, but she did learn to maneuver around muscle-headed football players and lecherous professors. It never involved in giving anything up, but convincing the problem male that there might to be the tiniest possibility. Men would do backflips if there were even a scent of action.

"Who?" Ronny eyebrows met as he tried to work out the mystery of who might be spreading his news.

"I'm not telling until you let me out." Time to bring out the big guns. "Sweet Cheeks." Her eyes checked the back mirror to make sure no one heard her. A black and white terrier watered a nearby tree, but he wouldn't be repeating anything.

"All right." He threw the truck in reverse so fast that the gears ground. Darcy shot out of her space and ran the stop sign. Her small, compact tires squealed as she made the turn too fast.

A lack of brains figured prominently into why Ronny and she would never be an item. That, paired with his desire to emulate the old television characters, *The Dukes of Hazards*, kept most women far, far away. Honestly, he wasn't bad looking. He was on the right side of forty and employed. Her mother accused her of being too fussy, but she didn't think so.

A couple hard right turns lost Ronny. Although, there wasn't too many places she could hide from the man if he wanted to follow her. He knew where she worked and lived. Ronny might be over the top whenever they met in public, but he never stalked her. His truck roaring up on the short street beside the library struck her as odd. Her nose wrinkled when she considered she didn't even know if Ronny read. She'd never seen him in the library.

The quandary of a smitten Ronny faded away as she turned into the apartment complex. A dented sedan indicated Lorna, her next-door neighbor, was home. The bright red pickup truck parked beside her car meant she had company.

In Darcy's designated parking place was Ruby's vintage VW bug convertible. In between humorous and sometimes offensive bumper stickers, a spot of blue showed. Ruby, her sometime friend, joked once that the adhesive strips were the only thing that held the car together. Back when she gave her friend a house key, it was supposed to be an emergency key. Ruby's key privileges came with checking on Sylvester. The few times she had to work overtime at Sweaty's, she'd called Ruby to check on her kitty. As far as she could tell, no evidence existed to prove Ruby ever dropped by when asked.

While her friend never showed up for cat duty, she did appear whenever she was between boyfriends or road trips. *Lucky her.*

Darcy parked her car while she mentally rehearsed the speech she'd use to get her house key back. Her apartment door swung open before she reached it. A shapely blonde attired in a peach low cut top and white short shorts that played up her tan, held up an oversized margarita glass. "Cheers. Come join the party."

Her jaw tightened as she reminded herself to get the key. Perhaps she could take it off Ruby's keyring after she passed out. "Hola, amiga." Since they had met originally in Spanish class, they both thought it would be clever to speak in Spanish as much as possible. "Que pasa?"

Ruby's shoulders went up in a shrug. "Ernie died. Heart attack. His kids blame me. They want to press charges." A sob interrupted her explanation. "I had no place else to go."

The fact Ruby's most recent elderly gentleman friend expired from trying to prove he was younger than the date on his driver's license didn't surprise her. "I was worried about the two of you trying to make a cross country trip on his touring motorcycle."

Ruby sniffed and chugged the rest of her drink. "We didn't even get past St. Louis. We were going to see this car museum after lunch. He bit into a triple bacon burger and fell out of his chair." Her fingers snapped to indicate how sudden it was.

"Was this before he ate the burger or after?" Darcy maneuvered around the woman into the apartment. Sylvester greeted her, then walked to his empty dish and meowed. "Ok, big guy, I hear you."

"It was before." Another sob absorbed whatever else said.

Personally, Darcy would have thought it would have been afterwards, but Ernie must have made a habit of devouring oversized greasy burgers. "That's too bad, but how did you get back here?" The Golden Almost Angels, senior citizen motorcycle group. stopped by the IGA for cold drinks. Ruby called her to tell her she turned in her cashier apron to follow the open road with Ernie. There hadn't been any mention of her aging vehicle.

"Bus. You know that big one that stops in front of the IGA. Mr. Oberson, the IGA owner, hadn't towed my vintage baby. I got off the bus, into my car, and came here."

Yay me! "I'm sorry about Ernie. I know you were fond of him." Ernie wasn't the first man Ruby helped to the other side. He could be dead boyfriend number three or possibly four. "Have you ever thought about men a trifle younger?"

Ruby snorted into the wad of tissues she'd grabbed from the box. "Mama always told me to go for the grateful men. That way they'd treat you well."

Darcy opened her mouth and then snapped it shut. Did she have any grateful men hanging around her? Nope, none, not a single one, although the image of the dark-haired stranger in the sports car appeared on the movie screen of her mind. No doubt the man missed the exit for the horse park or something. No reason someone like him would hang around here. Nothing to entertain an out-of-towner unless he came for the school bus double eight races. The event usually attracted several hundred people, including anxious mothers who wanted to make sure their child's bus driver wasn't a contender. Another handful of parents hoped their offspring's driver made it to the top three coveted spots. The winner received not only an oversized trophy with a dented school bus on top, but a year's supply of wings and beer at Sweaty's.

"Did you hear a word I said?"

Ruby's voice grated as Darcy popped the top of the cat food can. Sylvester's cries grew louder, perhaps afraid she might get sidetracked by her unexpected visitor. "Grateful men are better." Which summed up everything she pulled from the conversation.

"No." The woman placed a French tipped nail by her mouth while her eyes flicked upward. "Well, I mean, yes. Grateful men are always better, but I meant the part about Rhonda bringing in another roommate just because I took off."

It made sense. Rhonda rented one of the roomier town houses at the new complex across town. Her hairdresser's salary, even with tips, couldn't swing the rent alone. "Not surprised. No one knew if you'd ever come back."

Another high-pitched wail threatened to puncture her eardrums. Darcy pulled her friend out of the doorway and shut the door. No reason to wake Joel, who worked the night shift at the truck factory in the next town or Loretta, who made a habit of going out every night. Couldn't exactly call it work, all she knew was the woman could be a nasty drunk. It didn't bode well for her being all that pleasant when sober either.

The sob ended abruptly as the door clicked closed, making her question its authenticity. It wouldn't be the first-time Darcy had been played. The tequila could be putting the M in maudlin as opposed to actual sadness. The real reason behind Ruby's tears could be her failure to break free of the town once again. She shot the deadbolt with vigor. Ruby's failed attempt to escape the tenacious tentacles of small town life could have been her story, too. The major difference lay in the fact that Ruby did go places, whereas she only thought about it and did nothing.

The townspeople condemned anyone who tried to leave. Those who successfully shook the dirt from their shoes in a sprint to freedom never knew about this attitude or even cared. The general opinion of those who returned hovered between not smart enough to realize how good they had it in Monrovia to suspicion to why they failed to make a go at it somewhere else. Perhaps, that served as her main reason for not leaving. If she couldn't make it in Monrovia, how could she survive on a much bigger playing field?

The liquor bottles in her small cabinet clinked together as Ruby searched for the fixings of a new drink. Anyone who walked in off the street and saw the collection of tequila, whiskey, and vodka containers would think she had a drinking problem, but she didn't. For reasons, she couldn't fathom the bartender Rick usually tossed the bottles, even when a couple of fingers of liquor remained. Her original intention in removing the bottles when she took out the trash was recycling, which she did. Recycling resulted in the bottles ended up in her cabinet.

Since her writing muse chose to go elsewhere, she tried to indulge in the Hemmingway method of write drunk and edit sober. Apparently, the writer never had a laptop. All she had when she woke up from her experiment were several pages of the letter L. Not one of her better ideas, she shelved it with some of the other not so great ways to jump start her career.

Ice bouncing off the bottom of a glass meant another liquor mixing triumph for her morose friend. "I'll clear off the sofa bed for you." The reminder would keep her on again and off again friend from collapsing on Darcy's bed. Ruby mumbled something indecipherable.

The few extra hours of peace she'd gained from her unceremonious ejection by her library boss vanished as she alternately fed and comforted her friend. A television movie about some girl dying from a rare disease served as a babysitter while Darcy got ready for her second job.

Sweaty's ex-wife was the one who'd come up with the idea of putting the female waitresses in black short shorts with knee high socks. Her uniform was topped off with a striped referee shirt and a silver whistle. At one time, the imaginative ex had them tuck penalty flags into the minuscule pockets of the shorts. The trailing swatches of colors had tipsy male patrons always grabbing for them. While this was an amusing game for the drinkers, it resulted in several dropped drink trays. No way could a woman manage a heavy tray with people grabbing her flag. Several men used it as an opportunity to grab her ass too, which meant she'd been felt up by half the men in town without the benefit of a combo platter dinner date.

In a town where very few secrets survived, she found it odd that most of the women regarded Sweaty's female employees as little more than hoochie mamas. The male employees got a pass because they wore black slacks. Darcy suspected they'd still get more respect even if they did don a pair of skintight shorts. Heavily pregnant Donna Lyn graduated to dark maternity pants when her shorts turned into a black strip underneath her burgeoning belly. Not what most men wanted while watching the game and throwing back brewskis with the buds. It reminded them too much of their wives.

An extra five minutes on her makeup could boost her tip potential. She swiped the eyelashes with two coats of Get Up and Be Noticed mascara before she stopped. "What are you doing?" She addressed the surprised image in the mirror. "When was the last time anyone at Sweaty's looked at my face?"

Good question and one she couldn't answer. While she didn't have the attributes Ruby packed around, she could enhance what she had. Two cold rubber cutlets shoved into her pushup bra rounded out her cleavage even though she never really liked using the things since she heard horror stories about them popping out at inopportune moments. Her fingers buttoned up the shirt as she evaluated the display of skin in the mirror.

Too much cleavage would not only validate the term hoochie mama, but wouldn't earn her the money she needed. The male patrons could look all they wanted without buying a thing. One button left undone would work. While standing, nothing showed, but that one unanchored button demonstrated promise. Any boy over twelve knew if he could get a girl to bend over he'd get a boob flash. All Sweaty's patrons were over twelve.

Normally, Darcy avoided any provocative behavior, but today had been a day. Tomorrow, she might not have her library job, either. Then there were the felons in the library. How could they miss seeing her when she was the only employee there? All this worrying about the ethics of showing too much skin and staying employed would be a moot point if dead.

Chapter Two

THE PEELING WOOD columns on the porch barely supported the sagging roof. Killian shook his head, staggered by how the house had deteriorated since he'd seen it last. Had it been fifteen or twenty years? His lips twisted as he tried to remember. Back then, his Great Uncle Indiana remained among the living. The short, stout man had spent his early years as a rodeo clown. He entertained them with colorful stories and even acting out maneuvers that tricked the enraged bulls.

He couldn't remember why they stop visiting. His formidable great aunt would show up at family reunions, but usually stayed on the sidelines, giving their lighthearted antics a disapproving stare. The woman spent her free time slapping labels on them all as they wandered back and forth from the groaning buffet table. His cousins probably earned classifications such as *did not live up to his potential, married beneath her,* or *trying to validate existence by pushing out endless offspring.* By fifteen, he had excelled in baseball and had enough confidence for five teenagers in his six-foot body. His label probably read *headed for a big fall.* It never occurred to him someone would take advantage of his cocky attitude until it happened.

The powerful engine emitted a throaty rumble as he tapped the accelerator after he shifted to park. Foolish, showoff move, but it pleased him. Currently, the car was the only good thing that remained.

The nearby neighbor's curtains twitched, indicating a presence behind the fabric. As a stranger, he might rate a possible police call claiming he was casing the place.

Killian shoved the car into drive as he decided to investigate the town. The speedometer needle never reached forty as he circled the town square and the local businesses on the perimeter. Small towns often served as speed traps.

An insurance office crowded next to a shop with quizzical name *Notions* and a window filled with white teddy bears and angels. Hard to know what type of shop it was. All he knew was he wouldn't be entering it. There was a small discount store, a dry cleaner, and a thin, narrow office with a shingle that announced lawyer, nothing else. Cars were packed into the spaces at the end of the square where a newer building stood. Rock music thumped from the interior, and the enticing scent of frying burgers and onions floated on the air.

He sniffed with appreciation. His stomach rumbled on cue, reminding him that his last meal was hours ago in Ohio, where he stopped for a breakfast sandwich. Not a decent meal, his mother would point out, not that a burger, fries, and a beer would be much better. Still, Killian took advantage of an open parking slot. Outside the restaurant, he stared up at the name written in cursive Neon script, Sweaty's. Maybe he read it wrong. Must be Sweety's, which sounded better. Perhaps, a grandmother bedecked in a ruffle apron ran it, although, granny probably would never play rock music.

The noise reached deafening levels as he entered. Televisions mounted above the bar competed with the thumping bass of the music. Numerous patrons crowded the place and yelled their drink orders along with conversations. His shoulders tensed as another man bumped into him on his way out.

"Sorry, bro." The unknown man muttered as he strode to the door. Killian had already reached across his body for the shoulder upholster that wasn't there. Thank God for that, his rapid-fire reactions might have caused an incident in the sleepy town. His eyes squeezed shut as he took a deep breath, trying to quell his fight or flight response. His reaction veered to fight nine out of ten times. It would probably be best to leave. He exhaled and opened his eyes to an attractive brunette attired in a referee shirt complete with a silver whistle.

The woman smiled at him. "Can I help you?"

He blinked. Did he need her to officiate at a pickup softball game? The televisions, the bar, the name Sweaty's, and the bizarre referee outfit all added up to sports bar. It should worry him that it took him so long to add up the clues. Even though he took a bullet to the thigh, his brain took the biggest hit. He might as well give up his Man Card if it took him seconds to register the second home of most men, the sports bar. Killian managed a tight smile.

"Well, I was hoping to get something to eat, but it looks pretty crazy."

The woman wrinkled her nose. "It's a little bit, but most of the customers are drivers that popped in for the rally. The majority already settled up their bills and should be headed out to the track to warm up before tonight's race. I can get you a seat next to the kitchen if you don't mind?" She gestured with the hand holding her order pad to a small table against the wall and next to the kitchen door.

"Suits me." It did, since his back would be against the wall. He exhaled heavily, knowing he shored up the cop stereotype by wanting to have a wall behind him. He backed into parking places for a quick getaway too when possible. Not all stereotypical behavior was a bad thing. Some were more of a survival mechanism.

He allowed the cute waitress to lead the way while his eyes dipped briefly to how well she filled out her shorts. Killian brought his eyes up fast not wanting her to catch him ogling. Some labels he didn't want. At the table, the woman handed him a menu, but he handed it back.

No need to look when he knew what he wanted. He peered at her nametag, which was pinned to a noteworthy chest. Why did women do that and then accuse men of staring at their breasts?

"Darcy, I know what I want."

The woman shifted her weight on her feet and flushed a little, which puzzled him.

"What would that be?" She held her pen over the order pad.

"Burger platter. The biggest one you have with fries. Beer. Anything on tap, except light."

She dashed the pencil across the pad before reading the order back. "One Come to Daddy combo with fries and onion rings. Beer on tap." She lifted her eyebrows.

"Yeah. Sounds good. Not too sure about the name though."

His comment surprised a chuckle out of Darcy.

"Yeah. All the names could use an overhaul. Most of the regulars are too embarrassed to say the names and shorten them. The Come to Daddy platter becomes the Daddy Platter." She put her foot behind her to pivot and leave him behind.

"Ah, wait." He fumbled for an excuse to get her to stay a little longer and talk to him. When was the last time he talked to a woman when it wasn't police work? When had a woman ever seen him as more than a cop? "Can I see that menu?"

She handed him the menu and flipped a page on the order pad.

"I want the Daddy platter. Just thought I'd entertain myself reading the names since you mentioned it."

"Okay." She shrugged her shoulders and headed for the pass-through window.

As delaying tactics, his had failed spectacularly. People, mainly men, plowed through the open area. Some left; others went up to the bar either to chat with the bartender or to get another brew that the busy servers hadn't been able to process with the crowd. Even if he had gotten the woman to spend more time with him, it could have been the end of her job.

He had no plans on staying here more than a month. His original plan was two weeks, but his captain urged him to take his vacation days, too. Whenever an officer fired his gun there was always an official inquiry. When something goes horribly wrong as it did with him and Jake, there's plenty of bureaucrats and journalists stirring things up and questioning procedure. Yeah, he didn't mind being out of the public eye.

SHELLEY, THE OTHER waitress, nudged her at the service station. The woman grabbed wrapped silverware and leaned toward Darcy to comment. "See you got the unknown hottie. Snagged him while my back was turned."

"You were in the ladies room." She winked at the woman knowing she wasn't the least bit perturbed. "Besides, he looked lost, and I took pity on him."

"Ha! Doubt that man would ever look lost. As for taking pity on him, any other woman in this town would have dragged him home in the time it took us to talk about it."

Darcy cast a furtive look in the direction of Tall and Tasty, but a familiar female silhouette blocked her view. Ruby had been asleep or close to it when she left. While her outfit remained the same, she had curled her hair. Great, thanks to her pep talk the woman was about to gobble up the only new blood in town. Her heart squeezed a little bit. It felt like it grew smaller, making her the reverse of the Grinch whose heart grew larger, resulting in him being nice to everyone.

Shelley whistled beside her. "Ruby Cornstairs is back in town, and she's already on the new man, like fleas on the dog."

It didn't help that her coworker verbalized her thoughts.

"Why can't she see Bruce McCormick thinks the world of her? That man would do anything for her."

The information made her narrow her eyes. Shelley was Bruce's cousin, so she should know. As if hearing his name conjured him, Bruce walked through the entry wearing his short-sleeved dress shirt and clip-on tie, which befitted a bank manager. He called out greetings to the staff and friends before taking his usual seat at the bar. During the week, Bruce usually ate his lunch here since there wasn't anywhere else on the square. If he didn't mind the drive to the outskirts where the highway exits were, he could have his pick of fast food. At Sweaty's he could have his burger served up with a side of gossip.

A man across the room snapped his fingers. As much as she'd like to ignore that type of behavior, she couldn't. She squeezed past Ruby, bumping her in the process. Call her petty. It just wasn't right that some women gobbled up all the men. Apparently, even the men Ruby didn't fancy carried a torch for her.

Darcy gave the finger snapper his bill and took two more add-ons for beer from a nearby table. As she rounded the bar to put in her order, a plan formulated in her head. An amazing plan. If it worked as least one facet of her life would be better.

She held up her fingers indicated how many beers she needed, then crossed two fingers meaning the regular draft. The servers had to work out a code because it was almost impossible to hear anything when the place got hopping. Often customers pointed to photos on the menus. The regulars ordered the same thing, which posed no issues. Darcy moved closer to Bruce while Rick pulled the beers.

"Hey, Bruce." She injected as much warmth as she could in the few words. The man was five years older than her so they'd never been school friends, but she knew him in the manner everyone knows everyone else in a small town. She knew his family, his dating history, including the tale of Roberta Green who decided at the last minute to marry a soldier. The serious, soft-spoken man might not be Ruby's usual type, but at least he was younger and probably grateful, too.

"Hey, Darcy. Busy today, huh?"

"Ruby's back." She angled her head to where Ruby was standing still chatting up the new guy. Bruce craned his neck for a better look.

"You're right." He nodded as a wistful expression crossed his face.

Rick slapped the bar, interrupting their conversation. "Beer's up."

She held up her hand in acknowledgment. "Ruby's staying with me. The poor girl is all broken up and totally unattached. I bet she'd appreciate someone trying to cheer her up."

Confident that she planted her seed, Darcy picked up the beers. There wasn't anything else she could do. The rest would be up to Bruce. A shrill ding of the bell cut through the noise, signaling her order was up. Time to deliver lunch to the handsome stranger. Sometimes her job could be the pits. She smirked aware this wasn't one of those times.

She stopped by for a beer on her way to grab the platter. Normally, she'd have delivered the beer first according to policy since most men downed at least one beer before the food arrived. She turned, noticed the lack of Ruby, then the absence of her customer. No way, the woman could have worked that fast, but obviously, she had. Her shoulders sagged. This cinched it. It was now officially her suckiest day ever. She wouldn't even be able to go home in case they were doing the mattress dance at her place.

"Hey, is that my food? It looks good."

The warm baritone came from behind her. Darcy kept a firm grip on the tray as she turned to meet an interested pair of dark chocolate eyes. Ah, he hadn't left. "It is your lunch. I though you got tired of waiting and left."

"No. Washed my hands." He held out his hands as if for inspection. Her eyes roamed over the strong, capable looking hands.

"Yep, they look clean. Ready to eat?"

He slid into his chair and grinned up at her. "Very"

She placed the beer on the table first, then the steaming food plate. "There you are. Can I get you anything else?" Her eyes cut to the condiment basket, which appeared to be full. Occasionally, they went missing bottle of hot sauce, and she had a good idea who the culprit was. At least, this condiment basket hadn't been pilfered.

The corner of his lips lifted, revealing strong white teeth. One of the eye teeth stuck out a little more than the rest. Darcy found herself entranced by this inconsistency.

"I'd like if you called me Killian. I noticed you addressed the other customers by their names."

He wanted her to call him by his name. She rocked up on her tiptoes, then back down when she realized what she'd done. "Killian, it is. Not Killi, or Lian." She struggled to find some other diminutives of the name.

He laughed, took a sip of his beer before answering. "Good heavens, no. I suspected my mother named me after one of the dwarves in *The Lord of the Rings* trilogy, but I refused to go by Killi. Next, people will expect me to do movie quotes or songs from the book."

"It's not such a bad thing. I saw the movie, and Killi was hot."

Killian raised one eyebrow and held out his hands to his side as if daring her to comment on his wide shoulders that tapered down to a flat stomach.

The cook's gravely voice broke the moment. "Darcy, you're needed in the kitchen."

Seriously? The most exciting man she'd ever met was flirting with her, and she had to man the grill while Clyde took a smoke break. No great quips came to mind as she waved at Killian and then pushed through the kitchen door. The cook already had his smokes out.

"The one in the middle is well. The one near the edge is medium rare. They're served together, and the fries are almost up." The man slipped out the door before she could grumbled about anything.

Clyde had been taking smoke breaks as long as she'd been working there. Good short order cooks were hard to come by, especially with what Sweaty's paid. Darcy indulged the cook because it helped her get her orders a little faster. It would make more sense if the man took a break between orders, but he didn't. The rare burger received little heat from its edge position still she pressed it with the metal spatula feeling the firmness, almost there.

A good hard slap to the order bell provided Darcy with some satisfaction. Most of the regulars had learned to ignore the bells, bar slaps, or any other sounds associated with running the place. The entrance door opened, and the fireplug of a man she'd spotted in the library strolled in. She immediately ducked, hoping the man hadn't seen her. The backdoor slammed, causing her to jerk around in her crouched position.

Clyde's nose wrinkled. "Should I ask what you're doing?"

"Looking for my contact. It fell out." As quick answers went, it was the best she could devise.

"Let me help." He brought his sweaty self and tobacco smell to her side and stared down at the floor. "I don't see anything, but I imagine that it's clear."

Darcy stared at the tile wondering how long she'd have to stare at the floor before confessing she lied. It would only add to her reputation as a habitual liar.

"Where is everyone?" Shelley's voice had them both looking up.

Clyde answered first. "We were looking for…"

"What is it?" Darcy interrupted the man. The less lies the better. It would be hard to keep up if she kept making them up.

"Your boyfriend, Ronny, is here and refuses to let anyone else wait on him." Shelly smirked at her.

Her eyes rolled upward as she groaned. "You know he's not my boyfriend."

"Good luck convincing him that. Besides, he's a loyal customer. Doesn't run a tab and never starts a fight. All good qualities in a *boyfriend*."

There was no help for it. She always waited on Ronny since he'd accept no other server. On her way out she'd have to pass the delicious Killian and possibly the embittered felon. Who else would enter Sweaty's to enrich her day? Her fingers touched her hair, making sure no wayward tendrils escaped from her ponytail.

"Don't worry about your hair," Clyde advised. "True love never cares what you look like."

The twice-divorced cook wasn't exactly a romance expert. Still, he had more experience than she did. As close as she ever came to a relationship was her ill-fated romance with Roan, a law enforcement officer from the next county. His appearance coincided with his cousin's wedding. What she thought was the romance of the century turned out to be more of a pit stop for Roan. Instead of having the decency to tell her it was over, he stopped answering her calls, then changed his number. Her back molars ground together whenever she thought about the jerkwad. Her open palm slapped the kitchen door, sending it swinging hard into the dining area.

Killian's eyes looked intrigued as he bit into his massive burger. She marched past him before the man could swallow. At least, he had nice enough manners not to talk with his mouth full. Her eyes narrowed as she swept by the town's local crime wave. The lid rattled on her anger teapot somewhat close to blowing off. It would be hard to decide whom she'd want to slap first, Ronny or the pissed-off thief.

The visiting felon packed away the heartburn special with onions. He didn't even look up as she went by, which was good. It meant he didn't recognize her. Few people would associate her black striped sports outfit and pony tail with the conservative tea length dress she wore at the library.

Ronny Benson sat at his favorite table near the door, gripping a knife in one hand and a fork in the other. The patrons around him appeared mildly amused because they knew exactly what he would say. He'd said it every day for at least the 212 days since she started keeping track. "You look good enough to eat."

The words caused a few people to titter. As much as she wanted to roll her eyes, she didn't. Her boss pointed out that the man was one of their best customers. He also had family who were good customers. Occasionally the family bought a couple of kegs off Sweaty's too. *Inhale through your nose, count to four, and then exhale.* It helped some, but never as much as she wanted.

"I'm not on the menu as you well know. What can I get you instead?"

He placed his hand over his heart and pretended to be in pain. "I guess I have to make due with a Who's chicken basket with a double order of seam ripping beans and a diet cherry cola."

She pretended to write it down. "Got it." Clyde probably already had his food cooking since Ronny ordered the same thing every time. Rick pointed out the man came only for her since he never bothered to order alcohol. In some ways, that didn't make him such a bad prospect. Darcy had the unlucky privilege of seeing most of the town's male population three sheets to the wind.

The exterior door swung open again, causing her to tense in anticipation. Who else could come to brighten her day?

Her brother William entered all smiles. His latest girlfriend Elaine Cronin hung onto his arm and looked at him as if he were some form of god who came to earth. The whistles and backslapping drew her attention. Everyone loved her brother, but this level of excitement was even unusual for him. Rick the bartender waved at her.

"Come on over here, Darcy. You got to see this rock your brother put on Elaine's finger."

They were getting married. She stood shell-shocked, unaware her brother even had this in the works. She had no problems with Elaine. She suited her twin brother.

Ronny took the opportunity to jostle her arm. "Before you know it, you'll be an aunt."

"You're right." She didn't even have the energy to gripe at Ronny for touching her. William finished his engineering degree and had a decent job in the city about an hour away. In typical William fashion, he'd mentioned he didn't mind making the two-hour commute because he wanted his children to have the same wholesome childhood he had in Monrovia. The man could be a commercial for family values and small town life.

Instead of joining the crowd surrounding the joyous couple, she headed for the food window. Ronny's dinner was bound to be up. There would be plenty of time to congratulate the two. The milling people forced her to swing wide going by her library visitor. He waved her down. Her heart turned over for a brief second.

"I need hot sauce.

It started beating again. She reached over a couple finishing their meal at a nearby table, snagged their hot sauce and placed it on the felon's table without a word. It might be best to take a vow of silence with the way her stomach was jumping around. She got an extra-large glass for Ronny and chocked it full of ice before filling it up with diet soda. He'd interpret her actions as a declaration of undying love as opposed to her not wanting to see him the rest of the night.

Chicken basket was ready along with the beans. If she had the inclination, she could have told the man if he had a serious interest in her, he might want to lay off the beans. Three hours and she could go home. At least, she knew Ruby wasn't there with Killian. A quick sideways glance had the man waving at her. Did he want another beer or was he being friendly?

She lifted the platter with Ronny's dinner at shoulder level and skirted Killian's table. "I'll be right with you."

"No problem, I can wait."

The man was practically perfect. All she needed to do was shake off this funk. It should be no surprise that her brother was getting married. People called it precious when little girls pretended to mother baby dolls or used sheer curtains for wedding veils. No one knew how to react when William wanted to play bridegroom by dressing up in his miniature suit when not even six.

Darcy had never wanted to be part of the wedding game.

Ronny's dinner was delivered with minimal conversation. The man dug in demonstrating his hunger, which meant he didn't necessarily come to see her. An older couple in the back waved at her, the Johnstons, her parents' friends. No way, she could blow them off. They'd report such behavior to her mother who would give her the disappointed look next time she saw her. Despite her twenty-fifth birthday and being on her own for the last three years, did not cancel out the effectiveness of the disappointed look.

Assuming her pleasant face, she headed over to Marvin and Gloria Johnston. "I hope you both enjoyed your meal. Would you like me to signal your waitress for your bill?"

Marvin shook his head. "I know how much it is." He withdrew a couple of tens from his wallet while Gloria eyed her legs.

"It's shameful your boss won't let you wear pants. It bothers me."

"You and me both."

The woman shook her head and grinned. "Well, I doubt you'll be working here too much longer, especially since your brother is getting married."

Not sure how that had anything to do with it.

Gloria touched her hand. "You're next."

She and William were fraternal twins, which meant they didn't do everything alike. If they did, it would be peculiar. "I don't think so."

The woman cupped a hand by her mouth to stage whisper. "Weddings always make men wonder if they're going to spend their lives alone. It gives them the extra nudge they need to propose. It worked on my Marvin." Her husband grinned and nodded.

"I'll keep that in mind." She already knew she'd hear endless repetitions of *You're next.*

A quick glance at her watch showed she still had two hours and forty-three minutes left. Time stopped whenever her life went into the free fall mode, which was all too frequently. The crowd of people divided and separated to allow William and Elaine an exit. Her brother waved at her.

"Darcy, Elaine has something to ask you."

As much as her brother enjoyed playing bridegroom, no one ever had to ask for his hand in marriage. What else could it be? A niggling thought crouched on her shoulder, then stood and whispered in her ear. Elaine was the sole girl in a family of boys and didn't even have a single female cousin. It didn't help that her mother had taken off with the vacuum cleaner salesman years earlier.

Elaine approached giggling while gesturing with her left hand whenever she could. The large diamond caught the light and reflected it everywhere. Elaine would have to keep her hand flapping to a minimum as not to blind airline pilots.

The woman put her palms together in a prayer-like manner. "Will you be my maid of honor?"

Elaine's hopeful eyes were on hers, as well as everyone else's. It was the absolute last thing she wanted to do. Ronny belched in the background, forcing her to reprioritize what she didn't want to do. Maid of honor was now number two.

Her hesitation caused William to add, "Please."

Even growing up next to her brother didn't make her immune to his charm.

"Okay," she conceded "But, I have no clue what to do."

"Thank you." Elaine wrapped both arms around her and squeezed. "You're the best. William told me your mother could help, too."

Her mother? How could she had forgotten her mother's dream of being a wedding planner? Her mother started hinting broadly when Darcy turned twenty about weddings. It wasn't so much that she expected her daughter to marry. She just wanted to plan the wedding. At least her mother would finally get her wish. Too bad, Darcy wouldn't get hers. Elaine's tight embrace prevented from even twisting to see if Killian was still there. It was probably better if he wasn't.

Chapter Three

KILLIAN WATCHED HIS waitress march by him, her chin firm, and her eyes sparking. He half-turned, curious to see who set her off. A grinning man with a ball cap tilted back on his head teased Darcy, who had no choice but to take the fool's order, although she'd probably rather toss him out. Patrons at the nearby tables laughed and elbowed each other. The man's antics could be a long-standing joke. The woman had to endure the harassment to keep her job. He flexed his hands wanting to punch the grinning fool.

His eyes closed, as he inhaled, trying to get his warring emotions under control. The police psychologist suggested he had anger control issues. The woman had the nerve to suggest the real reason their fence operation failed had more to do with his lack of impulse control as opposed to an informant. He knew better.

Other voices joined the ruckus that provided the background. A few hoots and shouted congratulations forced him to open his eyes. A well-groomed man who could have posed for the cover of a men's fashion magazine had his arm wrapped around a beaming woman. Other patrons left their table to crowd around the couple. The men slapped the man on the back while the women bent over something he couldn't see. The unknown always rode him. His job was to evaluate the situation, then decide on his response. Right now, Darcy's actions intrigued him more. Despite, the couple of the hour calling her name, she darted to the food window.

Most servers would at least answer, but she wasn't for whatever reason, which made it even more of a mystery. He enjoyed a good intrigue, although most of his involved criminal cases. Darcy whipped past him with the loaded tray so fast he identified the contents only by the hot chicken grease smell that wafted behind. His gaze followed Darcy as she delivered the meal to the annoying man. She plopped down the plate and drink and left without any conversation.

Her hand went up to her neck. Another patron waved her down and requested something. Darcy stopped and snatched a bottle from a cardboard beer six-pack holder that did double duty as a condiment carrier from another table. The departing guests slid around her. The purloined bottle ended up on the man's table who'd originally waved her down. From her profile, he could tell Darcy didn't bother to say anything when she delivered the bottle. As cute as she might be, her abrupt behavior wouldn't earn her any tips. Her shoulders hunched forward as she headed for the kitchen.

Only minutes before, the server had been all smiles and joking with him, but something or someone set her off. Ball cap boy was chowing down on his chicken fingers, but his eyes stayed on Darcy. As annoying as the man might be, it appeared his pretty waitress avoided the happy couple. The male half of the couple shouted across the restaurant. "Elaine has a question for you."

Darcy stopped in her escape attempt only a foot from the kitchen door, her shoulders tensed as she forced herself to pivot to face the giggling Elaine. The crowd parted, allowing the attractive woman an easy passage to Darcy, whom she enveloped in a hug.

The woman's voice went up and down, but he could pick out words like *wedding* and *bridesmaid*. No wonder Darcy had made a run for it. The whole idea made him uncomfortable, but probably for different reasons. His sister, Shona, played the part of the bridesmaid four times. She insisted the brides always tried to make the bridesmaids look ridiculous in frumpy dresses. If that wasn't bad enough, according to his sister, the ugly clothing cost major bucks. Then, as the bridesmaids, they were supposed to plan different types of parties. He couldn't remember what they all were, except Shona muttered about it costing her a boatload of money that she could have spent on a primo vacation.

He watched as the woman tightened her hold on Darcy as if she'd get away. Another waitress brought him his bill and winked at him.

"Looks like Darcy is busy with her twin getting married and all. I'll settle you up."

The happy bride appeared to be overjoyed, when the groom joined them. His exuberant tone carried.

"Mother always has been a frustrated wedding planner. She'd love to help with the wedding."

Darcy groaned, still caught in what was one of the longest hugs on record.

Killian nodded at the happy bridegroom as he stood. A twenty rested across his bill on the table covering the tab along with a hefty tip, which he hoped Darcy received. Too bad, he couldn't talk to the attractive brunette again, but he knew where she worked.

Instead of heading out the front door, he veered down a narrow hall. A neon sign labeled the area, locker rooms. A pony keg held the back door open. Killian moved around it, skirted the building, looking for any other possible exits. Other people walked in and out of doors never giving it a second thought, while he always considered how to escape when a dead body or a gunman blocked the traditional exit. His attention to detail and paranoia had kept him alive.

Music along with loud cheers poured out of Sweaty's. He wondered what was said, but imagined it had something to do with drinks being free. The happy groom delighted at the prospect of his future life decided to treat the regulars. So much happiness rubbed on his nerves lately. He'd been in love once. He shook his head violently as if to shake the memory out of his head. His desire for a family, despite the anecdotal evidence that cops make lousy husbands, sometimes made him evaluate every woman as possibly *the one*. If Fate had been talking to him, he needed to listen harder. Apparently, Fate had said *the one to avoid*.

Killian dug into his pockets for his car keys. He nodded at a couple on the sidewalk who gave him a cheery *good evening*. There was nothing to worry about in this town, no crime, no backstabbing girlfriend out to ruin his reputation and career. In about a week or more, after he fixed a few squeaky doors and sticky windows, he'd get the phone call that would end his forced absence. Before he left, he really needed to do something about his aunt's porch.

ELAINE FINALLY LET go after saying how excited she was to be Darcy's sister. Clyde's belligerent bell ringing made her potential sister-in-law loosen her death grip and only after William pointed out that his sister needed to do her job.

A saucer of fries stacked high waited for her at the window. "Who ordered these?"

Clyde gave her a wink. "No one, but you looked like you needed a reprieve. Give them to Ronny. He won't even complain he didn't order them."

True, but her steps slowed as she passed the empty table where the handsome stranger had sat. He had an exotic name. Killium, Killian, or something like that. Not surprising he left after a display of Monrovian craziness. The town took its name from its religious founders who came from some area near the Czech Republic more than a half century before. Every child educated in the area endured a regional history class. The ornate Monrovian church no longer functioned as a sanctuary, but hosted a variety of businesses including a preschool, a catering business, and Mallee's Auto Supplies.

The local history lesson emphasized the church believed in unity, but disunity tore it apart, sending the settlers in a variety of directions. A few people claimed to be actual descendants of the founders, but the claims had as much validity of the genuine Monrovia star decorations sold in Wilson's Five and Dime store. The plastic stars came from China.

Nope. This wasn't a place where people stayed. Only those who no other option or ambition remained, which made her wonder which one she was. Darcy placed the plate of fries on Ronny's table.

"Compliments of the house." She was in no mood to argue about adding on another dollar and a half to his bill. Most people would have muttered their thanks and kept on eating. No such luck when it came to her self-proclaimed suitor.

His fingers fanned over his chest as he looked up in surprise. "Oh, be still my beating heart. My love has declared her affection for me."

The words surprised her. They were too lyrical to have come out of Ronny's mouth. Was it possible she underestimated the man? He could have deeper feelings for her than she ever expected. What was it about him she despised so much? Before she could explain the fries weren't from her, the man kept talking.

He pointed to the fries while projecting over the ambient noise. "The woman wants my body. She brought me free food."

A few men looked up from their pool game in the very back. Great, not exactly what she wanted, especially if the rumor of free food got back to her boss. Darcy would write out a ticket for the fries and pay for it. "They aren't free. Quit telling everyone you got free food." She pushed out the words behind gritted teeth and spun away. She grabbed the twenty and bill as she passed the empty table. All she had left of tall, dark, and delicious would be a generous tip.

Another glance at her watch indicated her shift wasn't anywhere close to ending. No matter how many emotions rolled through her, sabotaging her peace of mind, she still needed this job. Every hour meant money. Lord knows she needed every buck she could get. A middle-aged couple holding hands, sat down in her section. Chuck and Roberta used to be secret sweethearts back in high school. The families couldn't stand each other over some long-ago rivalry. Some people claimed it had something to do with land boundaries while others put it down to one of the original patriarchs messing with each other's wives. In the end, Chuck and Roberta married different people as opposed to each other.

Twenty-two years later, Roberta was a widow due to her husband being gored by their prize bull. The bull hadn't been on board with the plan to sell his frozen semen. Chuck's wife took off after seeing a traveling production of The Phantom of the Opera. Her secret dream must have been to act or to hang out in opera houses, hoping to meet a phantom. The door had barely banged shut after his wife's impulsive departure before Chuck showed up on Roberta's doorstep with an armload of tulips. It probably was as close to Romeo and Juliet as the town had.

Darcy smiled at the two romantics. Wouldn't it be wonderful to have someone gaze at her like that when she was forty? Her lips twisted to one side as she considered waiting years for such a miraculous occurrence. She handed the menus to the couple knowing good and well what they'd order. Love-Love, named as a nod to a scoreless tennis game, featured an oversized steak, two side salads, and two loaded baked potatoes. Few people ordered it knowing they had a better-quality steak in their freezer. The hefty price tag stopped the others. Besides, people didn't come to Sweaty's for romantic dinners. They headed up the road twenty miles to the Italian place that had candles in

Chianti wine bottles and cloth napkins. It also had the added benefit of not being gossip central.

Roberta touched her arm as she turned to leave. "What's up Darcy?"

The woman had been both her Sunday school and sixth grade teacher at different stages of her childhood. The concern in her inquiry touched her, but she knew enough not to confess anything, especially here where it would be repeated and embellished a few dozen times in the telling. Her shoulders went up in a shrug that said nothing. Then again it must have whispered something because Roberta squeezed her arm before dropping her hand.

"It gets better, sweetie."

Darcy fought her first response to reply, *maybe for you.* Instead, she managed a weak smile. What did better look like? She wasn't sure. When she was twelve, she took out her spiral notebook and mapped out her life inspired by all the talk of five and ten year plans. Instead of bullets, she used stars. At the grand age of twenty-six, her goal had been to have two books on the New York Times Best Seller list. Her daydreams included living in a penthouse apartment in the TriBeCa neighborhood with celebrities as her neighbors. Of course, she'd had a handsome spouse with some high-end job. Killian's strong features and ready smile superimposed themselves over the face of her dream husband who previously bore a remarkable resemblance to a boy-boy member. Included in her fantasy life was a darling dog that had to be walked by her personal assistant. Darcy had been clueless what an assistant did, but knew enough that successful people needed one.

Tempted to ring the bell, she slapped the order on the window ledge. Her hand hovered over it knowing the bell was the cook's property. Clyde wouldn't be pleased if she rang it in her funk. "Clyde, order."

A large beefy hand grabbed the paper.

Shelley waved at her from across the room. It wasn't the friendly type of wave that acknowledged the other person. Nope, it was the *I need you right here right now* gesture. Shift change, at least for Shelley, and no sign of Donna Lyn, which wasn't good. It would mean she'd be the only server for however long it would take Donna Lyn to show.

Shelley babbled as soon as she was within a foot of her. "I have a date tonight with Wayne."

At the mention of the woman's ex-husband, Darcy's eyebrows lifted.

"Yeah, I know, but we were thinking about talking things out." Shelley shuffled her feet as if line dancing.

Talking things out served as code for there was no date-worthy men in Monrovia. Might as well go with what you knew. "Okay." She didn't say anything else since she knew the results would be the same. If she complained about being abandoned, then Shelley would be pissy with her the next time she wanted a favor.

"I checked on all my customers. Two top in the back already has their check." She angled her head to baldie from the library, "I tried to give him his check, but he wanted to wait since there might be something else he wanted."

Oh, yeah. The man she absolutely didn't want to have anything to do with. It would allow him more time to study her face, not something she wanted.

"Oh, and you can keep all the tips too."

Darcy's eyes snapped back to the other waitress. "You must be pretty serious about Wayne."

Shelley nodded her head while her eyes twinkled over the hand she held up to her mouth. A small gap between her two front teeth resulted in always smiling behind her hand.

"I am. I didn't give him enough of a chance last time."

Since Darcy heard endless complaints about Wayne's boorish behavior. She'd have thought the woman gave Wayne thousands of chances to improve. What Shelley didn't realize at the time was most of the town's bachelors were just like Wayne or worse. The town's male population existed in some freakish town warp where women existed to provide hot meals and the appropriate number of children, mainly male.

"Go have fun." She took the proffered bills Shelley held out to her. Lucky her, she got grumpy and criminal. The man could camp out at the bar all night waiting for a return visit from the minister, who wouldn't make the mistake of stepping into the sports bar.

Her eyes followed Shelly, who smiled and waved at the regulars. She even mentioned her plans to see Wayne. The idea of getting back with her boorish ex turned Shelley giddy. The reason Darcy had no plans for the evening or the weekends was due to her inflated standards as her mother helpfully pointed out. If that wasn't bad enough. It served as a launching pad for the one who got away discussion. Darcy squeezed her eyes shut, hoping to prevent the memory from resurrecting itself.

A shadow loomed over her as a masculine hand cupped her shoulder.

"Are you all right?"

Darcy's eyelids flicked open to a close-up of Ronny's beard stubble. He angled his head downward allowing her to see his eyes. The man was tall. She had to give him that, and he did look concerned. More than a few single women in town would disembowel her with a hunting knife, if only metaphorically, because Ronny, one of the few employed bachelors, wouldn't consider any woman who'd welcome his advances due to his obsession with Darcy. Maybe she did expect too much.

Her focus went soft as she tried to imagine life with Ronny. The man was crazy about her and would probably do whatever she wanted.

Her granny always encouraged her to marry someone who loved her more than she loved him. The doublewide had to be more spacious than her cramped apartment. Perhaps she'd have time to write.

A loud belch broke her reverie. *Ah, yeah, right.* It would be better to be a confirmed spinster like her high school English teacher who announced one day she was a sixty-two-year-old virgin and proud of it. *I hope it won't come to that since it would be a lie.*

The sound of dated rock ballad playing along with the bell on the door announcing another customer sharpened her gaze. A few people gave her a curious glance while a couple of Ronny's buddies held their thumbs up at waist level. The males might as well have held up numbered cards as subtle as they were.

Ronny's breath brushed her cheek as he spoke. "You work too hard."

"You'll get no argument from me."

The cook bell sent out its shrill jangle, an order up or possibly a rescue. "Gotta get back to work." Darcy pivoted out from his hand, but before she could take more than two steps, Ronny shouted after her.

"You wouldn't have to work if you were my woman."

The words were probably meant to provide some comfort or enticement. They added to her public humiliation. At least, Killian didn't witness the scene, although as a non-local he would have people repeat a dozen different versions of the scene. One would have her swooning in Ronny's arms.

The local auto racetrack beefed up attendance with a semi-truck pull with the trucks substituting tractors. They also had mini-van drag races where mothers displayed their skills at burning rubber. The favorite was school bus figure eight races. The school buses would maneuver an eight-shaped track marked by yellow flags since they didn't have a paved track for this purpose. The fastest driver who completed the course without rolling the bus won. They had several heats since all the buses couldn't race at once.

A beefy man who arrived for the school bus figure eight called out. "I'd take that offer in a heartbeat if I had the right equipment." His hands curved over his chest, leaving no question of what he meant.

Irritated at the laugher that accompanied the man's words and performance, she responded with a touch of snarkiness. "I see you're still here. You'll miss out on drawing for the ATV. Only the figure eight participants can enter."

The man threw down a bill, grabbed his ball cap, and sprinted out the door.

Clyde met her at the pass-through window with a plate and an amused expression.

"You know good and well, there is no ATV giveaway."

"Yeah." As much as she tried not to, she wrinkled her nose, and smiled. "He'll figure it out once he asks someone."

After Ronny left, the rest of her shift passed without any interesting events. Mr. Felonious followed after him, making her suspect the man she always dismissed as being a little south of average intelligence might be a criminal mastermind. The villain was always in plain sight in the movies, but people always assumed he or she was harmless.

Dona Lynne came in thirty minutes late. The very pregnant server tapped Darcy on the arm as she squeezed by her to the shabby break room where they stored their purses in cast off school lockers. "Sorry, I was late. My feet have swollen so much I couldn't find a pair of shoes that would fit."

Darcy took a step back to see past the swollen belly. A bedraggled pair of terry scuffs with yellow ducks encased the swollen feet. "I guess you'll be comfy tonight."

"It's obvious you've never been pregnant. There's nothing comfortable about it." Exhaustion tinged her words.

Hard to know what to say. If she agreed, the server would point out once again that she'd never been pregnant. "Glad to have you here, though." Even though she felt guilty about the woman swaying around the room. Often, she carried her heavy trays, more often than not, a patron would pop up and carry it for her. While she might mentally lambast the residents for being too old school, occasionally the attitude could be helpful, especially when pregnant.

Since her shift started early, she'd have a few hours left before she went to sleep. The men crowded around the bar cheering on their favorite sports team. Darcy appreciated their team allegiance. The bartender served those at the bar. Whenever a table came into view filled with men drunk on alcohol and their combined testosterone, she made a wide swing around them. Early on, Shelley warned her once a man got a beer or two in him and was in the presence of like-minded individuals, their favorite game appeared to be grope the waitress.

Her first experience came when she had a tray heavy with drinks when a soused patron latched onto her left butt cheek. The sensation so alarmed her she dropped the entire tray. The owner was going to deduct the amount from her meager paycheck until Shelley talked him out of it. The culprit was a little old man she'd have sworn didn't have a lecherous thought in his head. Working at the bar taught her different.

Too bad the servers got the blame for the offensive behavior. There was no way she invited it. When it was super crowded, the smell of sweat and beer permeated the air. It also meant getting through the masses made her half roller derby brawler to get to her tables. It was then hands other than her own grabbed, pinched, even caressed her ass.

Any alternative had to be a better life than this. The thought needled her as she worked her way through the second wave of school bus figure eight participants. A few of them emboldened by a few brewskis hit on her. If a man was fool enough to hit on Dona Lynne, she'd accidentally spill his beer onto him. Everyone knew you never raised your voice to a pregnant woman, especially one already past her due date. It wasn't a matter of a courtesy, but caution, since said woman could attack with whatever was nearby. It had happened more than once, and the locals knew good and well not to cross Dona Lynne. The out of towners not so much.

Darcy kept an ear open for the inevitable slap, followed by a roar of outage.

"Why you little…"

The sound of dozens of chair legs scarring the floor as the local boys jumped up in defense of Dona Lynne drowned out whatever else the man said. A scrutiny of musclebound farm boys, along with a couple mechanics and Too Tall Todd McGraw who almost topped seven feet had the man murmuring an apology.

Well, that would be as much as an excitement as she'd see tonight unless there was an unpleasant surprise waiting at her apartment. Maybe she could volunteer to work the entire night.

Chapter Four

AN OLDER SEDAN sat in the driveway covered with bumper stickers, which surprised him since it must be his aunt's car. Killian slid out of his car, grabbed his duffle, and sauntered up the driveway, pausing to read a few of the bumper stickers. The first one read **Turn signals serve a purpose. Use Yours.** Hard to argue with that one. The next one read **If I wanted to know your hard luck story, I'd have asked you.** Whoa, harsh, good thing the print was small on that one. Someone offended by it might rear end her or worse. Another mention something about movies ruining books since 1897. "Looks like my aunt has some definite opinions."

It may also have been the reason he spent his time with his uncle the few times they had visited. His mother's prompting was the only reason he came. Most of her cronies referred to her as Saint Angela since she couldn't pass a lost child or a stray dog without helping. Often the dogs ended up at their house and never left voluntarily. There were a few owners who claimed their dogs, but that was a rare occurrence.

Their ten-acre plot of land served as an informal rescue dog retreat. Growing up, Killian not only had a dog or two to romp with. but puppies too. The biggest percentages of abandoned dogs were pregnant bitches, the canine kind. His father griped about the dogs from time to time but grudgingly endured them. He remembered overhearing his father explaining to a friend that his wife's habit of collecting strays was much cheaper than a shopping addiction. To aid in reducing the pet care costs, his mother bought vaccines at the local tractor and supply shop and gave the pack rabies shots at home. Since she'd been a nurse before she married, she must have had some shot expertise.

It was hard to understand how his compassionate mother had a close relative who had a critical opinion of almost everything and felt the need to share it. His hand tightened on his duffle. *Who thought this was a good idea?* Oh yeah, his mother.

Harry, a school friend, had invited him to use his fishing cabin, but Killian demurred. The last thing he wanted was to run into other cops while he was being investigated. Oh, they called it standard procedure, but he knew what it was. The worse part was it made him seem dirty and every single cop knew about it. Confidential didn't mean a thing. That was the real reason he was here. It would give him a chance to consider possible career options as he helped his relative.

The overgrown bushes could use a trim. Weeds poked through the cracks in the driveway pavement. The place needed help. It surprised him how fast the house had fallen in disrepair once his uncle died. His eyes moved upward past the sagging porch roof, which qualified as a safety hazard to the gutters that hosted a bumper crop of maple seedlings. Good chance his uncle hadn't been in any condition to be climb a ladder to tack down the lifted shingles. Could be he had too much pride to ask a neighbor for help.

A white-haired lady gripped a cane with one hand and the lead to a gray muzzled dog with the other. Could be that his aunt's neighbors were all as old as she was or possibly older. The woman catching sight of Killian, waved.

"Hello, there."

He inhaled deeply, pivoted, and made the few steps needed to reach the woman. "Hello. What can I do for you and your canine protector?" He dropped his duffle, squatted, and scratched the pooch behind the ears. A slight whimper and slow wag indicated that Killian had found the sweet spot the dog seldom could reach on his own.

"You must be Tish's nephew."

The shortened name didn't seem to suit his aunt, but the woman could have been a school girl friend. Who knew what his great aunt was like a long time ago? "I am. Name's Killian." He held out his hand, then dropped it when he realized the woman had no free hand.

"Oh no, you don't." She dropped the leash. "Colonel Mustard isn't prone to bolting." She held out her blue-veined hand. "It isn't often I get to shake hands with such a fine specimen of Black Irish. You remind me of the actor, ah." Her eyes rolled up as she tried to pluck the name from a forgotten mental filing cabinet.

Killian took the slender hand in his and very gently shook it. Early on, he'd been warned that the elderly valued handshakes as a proof of an officer's worth, but to be very careful not to squeeze and pain already arthritic hands. The woman cooed and giggled as he released her hand.

"Oh my! Can't remember the actor's name, but you are every bit as handsome. I'm sure the ladies of Monrovia wouldn't mind you hanging out and providing a well welcomed reprieved from the grizzled men of the town who stink of animal manure and car oil." The woman pursed her lips. "Not everyone is that bad, just those with their ball caps, failure to shave, and body odor that slaps you sideways."

His lips quirked up at the woman's honesty. There had to be a magic age when you could say whatever you thought without anyone thinking the worst of you. Hard to imagine anyone not liking the frail woman and her equally feeble dog.

The screen door slammed behind him.

"Johnetta Taylor, I thank you not to make a play for my nephew. He's fifty years your junior."

Whatever that age of sweet old lady, his aunt hadn't reached it. He knelt to pick up the leash for Johnetta who flapped her hand at his aunt.

"Pish-posh, don't get your panties in a wad."

He winced not even wanting to turn and see the outrage on his relative's face.

"Besides, I was thinking of my granddaughters. I have two that are still single, ya know."

A snort sounded behind his back indicating his aunt had moved closer.

"It's kind of hard to miss with the two of them knocking down the bridesmaids to grab the bouquet at every wedding."

Instead of acting offended by his aunt's summary, the woman gave a weary smile. "They are a bit too enthusiastic." Johnetta nodded in his direction. "They're good cooks."

"I'm sure they are." It wasn't the first time some well-meaning person tried to fix him up. Normally, it was his own relatives, usually his mother. At any given moment, his mother could supply him with the names of a half dozen of her canine-loving pals. Most of them sported T-shirts that read *I like to drink wine and rescue dogs*. While his mother thought both made for an excellent companion, he wanted something more like honesty. He handed the woman the lead and murmured goodbye. She trilled her greeting and made her halting way down the sidewalk.

He hesitated, not sure, if he wanted to greet the woman who upset so easily. *Suck it up, buddy.* His aunt did provide a place where he could lay low while awaiting the all clear signal to return to work. He closed his eyes to arrange his face in an affable pose. With elderly sweethearts like Johnetta Taylor or the hot waitress down at the sportsbar, it wasn't hard. No one had a clue how many times he'd stretched his lips into a smile and urged a person to either slow down, lower the music, or go home when he had something much different in the mind, especially when they return the kindness with rudeness.

Could be that his aunt would keep him in practice. Smile in place, he pivoted. "Evening, Aunt."

The frail woman didn't speak, but gave him a thorough look starting at his feet and swept upward. She gave a disdainful sniff. "You have the look of your father."

"Thank you."

The woman's eyes flashed behind her spectacles as she placed both hands on her hips. "I didn't mean it as a compliment."

Killian nodded, aware that her tone of voice had indicated as much.

His aunt cocked her head to one side regarding him the same way someone might regard a mangy stray that attempted to get into the house. "Your father was handsome smooth talker who swept your mother off her feet."

There were several photos around his family home of his parents together in their younger years. Often the smiling couple reminded him of old time movies stars with their dated clothes and striking looks. Growing up, they were simply his parents. Still, the pictures demonstrated how in love the two of them were. "They made a happy pair."

"Happy. Ha. What good does that do your mother, now?"

Easy, remember she's old, possibly senile. His policeman father, Sean, had been killed in the line of duty ten years ago. It decided Killian on the law enforcement path. Originally, he just wanted to hunt down the scum that killed his father. His only regret was his dad never saw him graduate from the academy.

Killian gritted his teeth to keep the wrong words from spilling out. "They'd had twenty-plus good years together, which is more than most people have."

The virago nodded her head in agreement. "Truer words were never spoken. Genevieve was always my favorite niece. The others didn't care if I lived or died. Your mother always stayed in touch with me via letter or phone, and more recently email. Forgive me, if I want the world to be a more pleasant place for her."

The angry lines in his aunt's face transformed into something resembling a smile. "I'd like it if you stayed if only for your mother's sake. I know it would disappoint her to hear you arrived and drove off all in the same day." She gestured back to her house with the sagging porch.

Ah, using his mother that was playing dirty. Killian studied his opponent. Make that relative. Good chance the woman was bitter because her husband died. He doubted anyone rushed to help her, considering how many people she ragged on over the years. "Yeah, Mom wouldn't be too happy with," he paused, knowing how his aunt would expect him to end the sentence, "either of us." Touché, take that, a direct hit with the guilt rapier.

"Come on in. I've made tuna casserole for dinner." She started up the front steps, but before she could reach the porch, Killian rush up the stairs and grabbed her arm.

"The porch roof could go at any time. Please use the backdoor, until I can get it shored up."

His aunt gave the roof a considering survey. "It is sagging more." She shook off his restraining arm and made her way down the steps and around to the back door.

Killian followed, realizing it must have just about killed her to accept help. His mother excelled in getting people to do what she wanted them to do while often making them believe they came up with the idea. Heaven knows she managed her manipulative magic on him more than once. He could remember cleaning out the garage when he was twelve wondering why he volunteered for such a dirty job.

Then there was Helena, his mother's most recent attempt to match him up. Mom never played fair. Her invitation mentioned her delicious lasagna, but nothing about bland Helena who worked at the local library. The woman kept trying to talk about noteworthy classics to him and expressed horror when he admitted he hadn't read *Middlemarch.*

Most people would have changed the conversation, but not Helena. She went on about his lack of literary education, then proceeded to quote the book. The woman had memorized it since it was one of her favorites. For him, it was up there with the root canal where the Novocain wore off before the procedure did. Yeah, the memory had him turning down all dinner invitations since his sister Shona warned him of impending match-ups. His mother's fatal mistake was sharing details about the perfect woman with his sibling.

His aunt swung open a creaky backdoor that Killian put on his mental to-do list. She held the door open for him, earning some extra points in his mind. Women seldom give men the same courtesies they naturally expect from holding doors open or even picking up dropped items.

"Thanks." He caught the door and walked into a kitchen that could have modeled for a dated sitcom with its harvest gold appliances and aluminum cabinets. The long windows allowed the setting sun to filter into the room and illuminated the chicks and hen wallpaper. Killian tried to remember the last time he'd been in the kitchen. Even though his memory was fuzzy, he'd bet nothing had changed.

The fragrant scent of tuna, cheese, and onions permeated the air as his aunt lifted a casserole dish out of the oven. As a kid, he'd made the mistake of complaining about all the various casseroles his mother routinely served. She explained that the casseroles stretched the food budget to feed growing boys like himself. Killian made a mental note to contribute to the food budget or at least take his aunt out a few times. "Does Monrovia have many restaurants?"

His aunt sent him a narrowed eye glare. "Planning to leave before you even taste it?"

"No, ma'am." He'd have to be on his toes not to get his aunt's back up. Luckily, she still had a full-time job that would keep them out of each other's way. Weekends might be a little more problematic. "I was thinking of some way to pay you back. I thought dinner in town might be nice."

"Ha. You got me there." She placed the casserole on a trivet in the middle of the table. "Can you get the ice tea out of the fridge? I'll get the plates."

By the time, the table was set and they both were seated, Killian assumed his aunt forgot the restaurant question. Rather than mention it again and possibly bring attention to a slipping memory, he decided to research it on his own. After a brief grace, his aunt ladled out the casserole, giving him an enormous helping. On a good day, when he hadn't already devoured a third pound burger and fries, he'd still have issues with packing it away. He picked up his fork determined to do justice to the meal.

The first bite sat in his mouth until he forced himself to swallow and follow it with a big gulp of sweet tea. His relative watched him attentively, which meant he had to eat more. Where was the family pet when you needed one?

"My husband loved my tuna casserole."

Killian found that hard to believe. "Was he a big fish fan?"

Her brow puckered as if trying to decipher something. She finally shook her head no. "Indiana didn't care for fish, but he was a big salt fan."

Well, that explained it. That could have hastened his jolly uncle on his way, too. There probably wasn't any way to get his aunt to lighten up on the sodium. There had to be another option. "This is all so good, but I need to drop some weight. The force has us on strict weight regulations"

"I find that hard to believe. What about all the jokes about cops eating donuts?"

Nothing would be easy with his aunt. He managed a smile before swallowing another bite. By tomorrow he'd be five pounds heavier just from bloating. "Some restaurants and donut shops would provide free meals, coffee, or donuts to have a police presence. It scared off any potential robbers. Not too many do that anymore. At best, we can get a free cup of coffee, which is welcome on a long night."

"That's a shame. Everyone has gotten so penny-pinching. Doesn't matter here though, since there's no place for you to eat except a pizza joint on the edge of town. It's closed more than it's open due to being family run. Whenever I go by, there's a sign up that it's closed due to a wedding, vacation, illness, or death in a family."

That didn't sound like much of an option, and he wasn't even sure if his aunt liked pizza. "What about that place in town. I think it was oddly named Sweaty's." He managed to act confused about the name as if he hadn't just come from there.

"Disgusting." His aunt stabbed at her plate. The fork tines made a horrendous sound as if adding its opinion of the place. "Horrible place. Men go there to watch sports, drink beer, and ogle the half-dressed waitresses."

The referee shirt and knee socks didn't rate up there with other sports bars he'd been in, but the tight black shorts had potential, especially the way Darcy filled them out. Now, he wouldn't have considered what he did was ogling, but maybe his aunt would. The friendly air of the place reminded him of the family pubs he'd visited on his last trip to Ireland. No need to mention any of it to his aunt, either. She came from the other side of his family, the non-drinking side.

"Well, I guess I won't be taking you to Sweaty's, then."

His aunt's posture grew rigid as her fork paused on the way to her mouth. "I should say not. I would not step into that place at gunpoint. Nothing good goes on there. No one decent is inside. Someone should burn the place down."

Killian hid a grin behind the tea glass. There were two definites in his life. The month would be extremely long, and he'd be spending a lot time at Sweaty's. With any luck, he might see Darcy again.

Chapter Five

DARCY HUNG UP her apron more than ready to leave. The owner wasn't in the habit of paying overtime. When questioned about it, he pointed out that the person who stayed got additional tips.

Clyde held up his hand in greeting. "Go out and do something fun for a change."

Somehow, Darcy pressed down the urge to laugh, knowing the cook meant well. "I'll take that under advisement." It would go under the file labeled **Get a Life**. Even though her feet hurt from walking miles across the hard cement floor, she hesitated at the back door. Her apartment wasn't the sanctuary it normally was with Ruby's impromptu arrival. The woman could teach squatters lessons in landing a rent-free bed.

"See ya." Darcy slipped out the door before she'd even heard the cook's reply. The streetlights provided a measure of security as she wove her way through pickup trucks and SUVs. Not that Monrovia had any type of crime. About the worst, they had was wannabe meth producers, who slipped into fields to steal the anhydrous ammonia tanks the farmers had bought to fertilize the fields. A few that either didn't have a hitch to move the tanks or didn't need an entire tank tried tapping into the tanks with a drill. The explosive result usually had the potential drug lords showing up at the local medical center where the sheriff greeted them.

Even crime didn't visit Monrovia. Darcy pursed her lips. *Make that not until today.* What a shame there was no one she could tell about the minister's shady past. Her brother, who normally had time for her, probably wouldn't even hear her, too lost in fantasies of his upcoming future. Life unrolled exactly the way William planned it. She clicked the fob on her keyring trying not to resent her brother's good fortune. How could they be twins and be so different.

A warm breeze rattled the tree leaves, which crackled, signaling fall was on its way. She slid behind the wheel and closed her door, which creaked as if it would fall off. What else could go wrong today? Would Ruby even be at her place? With any luck, the woman would be out looking for her next *boyfriend.* There had to be some aging Romeos over at the speedway. Ruby fared better with the men who never thought they had a chance.

The car engine moaned, coughed, and caught the third time. *Thank the Good Lord.* Her held breath escaped with a whoosh. One more thing would send her over the edge. Not sure, where she'd go if she made that final jump, but the edge kept getting closer and closer. All she wanted to do at this point was take a hot shower and wipe off the ickiness deposited by various male hands that somehow ended up on her legs, hips, arms, even the side of her boobs. Normally, the tray protected her from frontal assault.

By this time, she knew who the touchers were and avoided them. William announcing his engagement along with the figure eight bus drivers crowding into the place produced chaos that a few took advantage of to slide their hands where they didn't belong. Darcy didn't take this lightly, swatting them with the tray while cursing, which only made them laugh. Probably the reaction they wanted, especially since a couple of them had asked her out, and she'd refused. For the price of a beer, they could take liberties she would have discouraged on a date.

The car headlights picked out the apartment sign the same time her stomach growled. Most restaurants allowed employees one free meal from the menu. Sweaty's allowed the employees one burger as opposed to a platter. Clyde usually fixed himself one for break and another to take home. He would have fixed her one as well since he knew no one kept close tabs on the inventory. His rationale involved being underpaid and overworked. Darcy would have taken it, if she hadn't been paranoid about the owner catching her.

The katydids' hum greeted her as she opened the car door. Her fifth-grade teacher had told the class only the males made noise to attract a mate. The low roar meant there had to be tons of available males trolling. Insects had a livelier love life than she did.

Darcy directed her gaze at the nearby trees trying to spot the elusive bug. Most people found the insect and its song annoying, but in a way, she admired it and the vilified cicada. The hard-shell beetle went to ground for several years only to miraculously emerge thirteen to seventeen years later. What did they dream of in their long underground time? Right now, she wouldn't mind vanishing into another world only to reappear years later as a reincarnation of her former self if only in the need to prove she wasn't the weirdo most of the locals considered her. A fancy car and a hot boyfriend might not change the town's opinion, but it would certainly help her esteem.

A reedy soprano singing about car tires on a gravel road meant her apartment wasn't empty. A couple of male voices talking stoked her irritation. She shoved the key into the door and twisted it open ready to stomp out whatever party occurring in her absence. Ruby stopped singing and glanced up in surprise. Her right hand clutched a bottle of flavored rum. Darcy's eyes surveyed the tiny apartment. No lurking males unless she considered her cat who tilted his head at her, which meant *humans be strange.* The television sound increased as a pizza commercial featuring a prancing man in a pizza delivery uniform, came on. The male voices must have been the television. *Now, didn't she feel stupid?*

A glassy-eyed Ruby stared at her with her bottom lip trembling. Obviously, the beauty had struck out tonight. No luck with tall, dark, and delicious. The realization cheered her. Yeah, she knew it was petty to take pleasure in the fact that Killian chose to pass on Ruby's bounteous charms, but hey, she was human.

"Hey, Rube, what happened?" She expected the details about the encounter between her and Killian.

The woman brandished the bottle. "Need a drink?" Before Darcy could answer, Ruby poured two fingers into a used glass and held it out to her. Normally, she didn't consider herself overly fussy. Drinking straight liquor out a dirty container pushed it a little, but the alcohol should kill any germs. Her fingers wrapped around the glass, and Darcy held it close to her lips as if sipping. Perhaps her playacting would serve. Ruby jumped to her feet and swayed a bit before she placed the bottle on the coffee table.

"Bottoms up, sister."

Ruby lunged toward Darcy, hitting the glass, which splashed its contents onto Darcy's face. She squeezed her eyes shut, trying to stop the slow burn. Irate, but trying not to show it, Darcy inhaled before asking. "What in the world caused you to do that?"

"William is getting married."

"Yes, I know. Where you at the bar when he came by?" It would be hard not to know her brother's impending nuptials in a small town, but she didn't see why it would upset Ruby. Could be she felt left out as Darcy did when another contemporary married. Then the proverbial light bulb lit up over her head. "Ruby."

Her friend picked up the rum bottle and chugged it as if were a beer. Ruby slammed it back on the table, causing the remote to dance across the veneer. "What?" Her whiny tone turned a touch belligerent.

"Did you…" Wow, she had no clue how to discreetly ask. "…and my brother." Not being able to get the words out, she formed her left thumb and index finger into a circle and plunged her right index finger in and out a few times.

"Girl!" Ruby slapped her hard on the back and stumbled backwards, forcing Darcy to wrap an arm around her friend's waist to prevent her from falling. Once Ruby regained her balance, the boozy blonde made her way to the sofa with some assistance. "I wish. Your brother never even looked at me."

"I find that hard to believe. There wasn't a male in Monrovia who hasn't lusted after you, especially since your breasts arrived before any of the other girls." Darcy glanced down at her modest cleavage. "I though mine must have been on special order from Timbuktu."

"If he had bothered to stare at me, it was only in disgust because I wasn't good enough for him. All he saw was trailer trash." Her elbows rested on her knees, and her hands cradled her head. Sobs and hiccups floated up.

Oh, great, a drunk friend who was sweet on my brother. Her earlier intentions of showing Ruby the door disintegrated. She'd have to give the woman time. What type of friend would she be to drop kick the brokenhearted female?

"That's so not true. William isn't like that. Do you even remember him treating anyone differently because of how much they had or didn't have?"

As much as she hated to admit it, her brother's innate goodness made her appear mean-spirited or just a little left of oddball in comparison. If she had a less noble sibling, maybe she would shine in contrast.

The crying stopped. Ruby lifted her head, blinked, and made a round O with her lips. "Do you think," there was a small catch in her breath, "that William could have ever been attracted to me?"

On the outside, it was a no brainer question. What woman wouldn't want to think she was attractive? Still, there it hung in the air with all the menace of unexploded firework. "Of course, he did. I even heard him mentioned it to his friends."

"Oh!" Ruby brought both her hands to her mouth, leaving the devil rum alone.

What she'd heard was that William agreed with his guy friends that Ruby did have the most bodacious tits in the county. It would be a betrayal of her brother to repeat it, and it would reveal her role as an eavesdropper. The last she was trying to live down.

Just when the emotional firestorm had bubbled down to a slight sniff, Ruby uttered a small screech and broke into sobs once more. Darcy stared at her friend's heaving shoulders unsure if she'd said something or the liquor managed to exert a final hurrah. "I told you William liked you. He thought you had bodacious tits." The last part she hadn't meant to say aloud. Once a woman heard something like that she couldn't help wondering if every man checked out her rack when she walked by. For the most part they did, but the ick factor was in the knowing.

"That's it!" Ruby managed to choke out the words.

She was too tired to translate Ruby's nonsensical remarks. She squeezed her eyes closed and could hear the siren call of her bed. Tomorrow would be another day, and she'd have to be on her best behavior if she wanted to charm Leticia into letting her keep her job. "Okay, Rube. I don't get it." She was ready to add she was going to bed, but her friend jerked her head up.

"If I knew he liked me, then I could have done something. We could have ended up being sisters."

The flip side would be that Ruby would have William to go home to and wouldn't be crashing at her place, which had merit too. Of course, that would depend on William liking Ruby as opposed to admiring her rack. It had been years since she'd overheard the comment. Her brother could have changed his mind about that, too. What would Ruby want to hear? She scoured her memory of various rom com movies she'd watched.

"Ah, William, he would never approach you. He was too in awe. My brother never aimed too high. He went for the sure thing." She crossed her fingers, hoping wind of the conversation never reached her future sister-in-law.

Ruby chewed on her bottom lip, possibly concocting daydreams of a lovesick William. If nothing else, the girl would have good dreams, which was something Darcy wouldn't mind. If she were lucky, a certain non-local hunk with an Irish name would star in hers. She sauntered down the hall to shower and get her romantic dream life going.

"It's not too late." Ruby's voice carried a note of excitement.

If the woman thought she would doll up and troll for available man candy, she needed a reality check. Monrovia rolled its sidewalks up at nine pm. Any available men in town had jobs that had them getting up at dawn or earlier. Ruby would do better to go asleep and get up early. Since Darcy's goals never included landing a farmer, she had no clue where they might be in the mornings. Possibly milking the cows or out in the fields. The feed store could be her friend's best bet.

Darcy backtracked to the living room where her friend had cleared the coffee table of all liquor and wrote feverishly in a spiral bound notebook. "What' cha doing?" As soon as the words were out of her mouth, she could have slapped herself. In a few brief seconds, it took to walk down the hall, she could have stripped, jumped in the shower, and scrubbed away the stress of her day. Curiosity or compassion sent her sniffing back.

Ruby paused in her writing and glanced up. Her eyes had that crazy shine that had people backing up in the movies. Darcy stumbled back a step.

Her friend held up the open notebook that had numbers marching down the page along with scribbling beside it. "I'm making a plan to get William back."

You never had him. She didn't bother to say the words because it would be work to convince Ruby otherwise. With any luck, she'd pass out on the couch and forget about the scheme. "All right, I'm heading to bed."

Her feet took her to the bathroom where she would treat herself to a nice, leisurely hot shower. Even the thought made her groan with pleasure. Darcy cranked on the water, unwilling to examine too closely that water was the only thing hot in her life currently. Once the water warmed, she stepped in the stream and wetted her hair thoroughly. A squeeze of the shampoo bottle produced a glob of green apple scented shampoo. Normally, she showered in the morning since her apartment shared a water heater with a next one. The actual obtainment of hot water practically became an art form with her listening to see when the shower came on in the next apartment. Lydia, her neighbor, was a late riser, which made the morning shower idea. Tonight, though, she worked her hands through her sudsy hair.

The steam vanished as the water turned. Darcy jumped out, swearing as she slipped, but caught herself on the towel rod. The shampoo burned her eyes as she stood looking at the towel rod she half pulled out of the wall. Maybe she could fix it. Yeah, right, she'd put it on her ever-increasing things to do list. Right now, she had to rinse her hair. Darcy sucked in her lips, tensing her body for what she knew would be icy water.

Tomorrow had to be better, didn't it?

Chapter Six

KILLIAN LOCKED HIS hands behind his head and stared up at the ceiling. He couldn't sleep. Not too surprising, considering everything that happened to him. Before he left the city, his sergeant told him to sit tight, and it would blow over. Easy for him to say since he wasn't the one everyone considered a dirty cop.

A sour, bitter taste rose in the back of his throat. His doctor insisted it was acid reflux, but he knew it was disgust at how easily he allowed himself to be manipulated by a woman with a hidden agenda. A desire to shower overcame him, but getting up in the middle of the night would only end up with his aunt peppering him with questions. Five minutes with his aunt made him understand why they quit visiting her. Still, he should know better than anyone else that there is always another side to a story.

The woman had night-lights plugged into every room. The ever-present glow made it hard to sleep, but may have provided some reassurance and made the house easy to navigate at night. Numerous locks on the exterior doors were more suitable to living in the projects than sleepy Monrovia. The last crime wave that hit the town was when a dozen senior boys thought it would be great fun to switch license plates. No one noticed for weeks since few people memorized their plate numbers. Not much of a prank, not like when he was in school.

His lips tipped up as he remembered his senior year at Our Lady of

Providence. There was no way his mother would have allowed him to attend school with heathens as she referred to all the non-Catholics. Of course, it only showed how naïve his mother was about how much Catholic schoolboys drank and their persuasive ability with the opposite sex. Life was so much simpler then. The pinnacle of his hell raising was the three little pigs stunt.

He and his buddies snuck into the school after hours with three greased pigs, which they had labeled one, two and four with a permanent marker. There was no three. Monday served as his first real test of keeping the brotherhood code by keeping an absolute straight face when a tiny porker shot by. The maintenance crew spent several hours searching for the animals. Once they captured three, even more time elapsed in pursuit of the mysterious number three pig. All the students agreed the three pigs prank ruled, but no one took credit for it. No one could since the principal threatened to withhold the pranksters' diplomas. Then there was the fact, he'd used his mother's keys to get into the building.

Identifying him would have cost his mother her beloved teaching job. Yeah, his mother escaped only because more than one staff member had a senior child. Half a dozen parents could have been lax with the school keys. Father Mike probably questioned the parents since the school foolishly believed people couldn't lie to priests. He wasn't sure if it was supposed to be a major sin or you ran the risk of a lightning strike. Plenty of kids lied in confessional knowing Father Mike would recognize their voices. As for the school, cameras ended up on all the doors. Back then, he set the pattern where his screw-ups often hurt those who mattered to him.

His lips firmed as he considered the possibility. Never his intention, then or now, but unless a person lived on a deserted island people surrounded you. The closer they were to you the more harm you could inflict. His infatuation with Heather and wanting her to be his storybook romance made him no better than a middle school girl who thought wishing for something hard enough could make it happen. His desire to settle down caused him to ignore his partner's warning that there was something not quite right with the woman.

His casual mention of Jake's comment to Heather probably caused his death. The fact Killian still breathed, he didn't put down to sentiment, but rather his guardian angel. His grandmother insisted he had one to be able to survive his various adventures as a boy. Still, he'd swear he heard his father's voice telling him to hit the ground. That tidbit he didn't share with the police psychiatrist. If he had, they'd think he was both crazy and dirty.

Nope, he could understand their suspicions. Most people called police cynical or paranoid. The fact he survived while his partner didn't convicted him without an official inquiry. Never mind the bullet he took to the thigh. That could just be part of the cover-up. A long sigh escaped his lips. *God dammit, he should have been smarter.* There were plenty of stories about cops led around by their dicks. He'd sworn he'd never be one of them, and now he was.

His stomach heaved and made an awkward roll. Killian sat up, unsure if he'd have to sprint to the bathroom down the hall. It could have been the greasy burger, but more likely, he swallowed way too much regret. His thoughts strayed to a dark-haired waitress named Darcy. *Talk about a tasty diversion.* His stomach relaxed enough to allow him to recline again.

Getting to know her wouldn't be fair to her, though. Girls who live in small towns like Monrovia expected the husband, house, and two kids. Surprising, she wasn't married. Could be divorced, which would explain her working at Sweaty's. Most men would not be okay with their wife or sweetheart working at a sports bar, aware the men would be ogling her and some would proposition her. Only a loser who refused to protect his woman would be okay with it. Sure, the woman might insist on doing it, but it would still be up to the man to do everything in his power to protect her, even if that meant glaring at anyone who put a hand on her rounded backside.

Sleep gradually weighted his eyelids as he considered the innocent charm of Darcy. No way a small-town girl could do a number on him the way Heather did. Yeah, maybe he'd been looking for love in all the wrong places.

THE STRIDENT RING of Darcy's alarm clock resulted in Ruby moaning. "Turn it off. Turn it off, now!" A half roll brought Darcy close enough to the offensive clock to shut it off. The water spot on the ceiling stood out like neon in the strong morning light. She never asked how the stain happened, didn't want to know. The story would be unsavory considering the apartment location on the seamier side of town. A former tenant could have murdered his spouse and amorphous blot happened as the result of him over soaking the floor above her apartment in an effort to sponge up the blood.

She blinked. She didn't know why people said she had an overactive imagination. It could have happened. Yesterday she spied two crooks in the book stacks, and one happened to be her minister. No one would believe her. If she could tell someone, then at least there would be a clue if her dead body showed up in the river. Well, that would involve having a river. It might pop up in the high school pool, which would involve breaking into the school. Her lips twisted as she realized the best she should hope for was one of the display troughs in front of the feed store. Her nose crinkled, not exactly a storybook ending.

She half-whispered to herself. "I'm going to do my best to avoid that."

"Do what?" Ruby gave a whimper. "Why do you have to yell everything?"

"I didn't yell. Oh, never mind." It was tempting to shout the words, knowing what a glass head Ruby had after chugging half a bottle or more of spiced rum, but she didn't. Unrequited love was a bitch, not that she would know. There never was anyone to crush on in Monrovia. Reason three she needed to leave.

Darcy had numbered all the reasons it was past time to head out to parts unknown. Her number one reason being that most people thought she was crazy. Of course, she might have to bump that down to two if felons trying to kill her replaced it. Number three was both the reason she was still in town and needed to leave it, no money. A long sigh escaped her lips. If cranky Mrs. Blankenship didn't keep her on at the library, she'd have even less money. This called for desperate actions, and she had just the disguise too.

At the back of her closet, was a knee length skirt, a pressed white blouse, beige cardigan and a pair of sensible loafers. The only thing missing would be reading glasses hanging from a beaded band. The idea to dress like her boss occurred to her after reading about how people tended to favor people who looked like them. With any luck and a dozen hairpins, she arranged her hair into an old lady bun. It might be enough to confuse the local crime wave and anyone else who came in as well.

"Ah, I need now is those clear lens glasses from high school."

Darcy stood ready to morph herself into a younger, less crabby version of Leticia Blankenship. A pounding on the wall meant Ruby objected to her speaking again. The woman would have to get used to it if she was going to crash here. Still, she'd try to keep quiet, but she couldn't say the same for Sylvester who mewed his request for food.

They both ignored a half-hearted whimper as Darcy switched on the kitchen light. She managed to feed her pet, start the coffee, and even located her fake glasses in the utility drawer without saying a word. While in high school, she tried out several different personalities including smart girl geek with her fake specs. No one took her seriously, including the teachers.

People naturally assumed the tall, good looking twin would be the sharpest one. Her kinder teachers mentioned her rich fantasy life on her permanent record. The not so kind wrote things such as flighty and irresponsible. No one even considered for a heartbeat that she helped William with his written essay. Maybe she sucked at math and chemistry, but she could write.

Dressed in her mini-me outfit she hoped would earn her points, she grabbed her coffee cup before waving to her cat. She tiptoed past her neighbor who was just coming home. The woman did a double take and then gave her a wry smile.

"Role playing, I see."

What her neighbor assumed was miles away from what she was really doing. "It's a new image for me."

"Ah, well." The woman nodded, not adding anything else.

Just as well, she didn't want to explain, especially since it might not be her most inspired idea. First, she'd have to see how it worked. She managed to get into the car without spilling her coffee, a plus. She started the car only to see the gas gauge drop to E. "Really?"

Her car clock showed she had only twelve minutes to get to the library, which was enough time if she didn't stop for gas. What did William tell her about the gas gauge? Something about it having at least a gallon in reserve even when it read empty? Enough to get her to the library and to the filling station later. Mind made up, she shifted the car into gear. "Please God, let today be a good day." The way things had been going it wouldn't hurt to get everyone in on the action. "Ah, Mother Nature, I could use some help here. Been keeping up with my recycling. Thought you might want to know. Still driving my fuel efficient compact. Appreciate anything you could do on my behalf."

Her rearview mirror shimmered and shook as she bumped into the library lot. Was there anyone else she could implore for some much needed help? Did she know any other deities? "Ah, Thor, you may not know me, but I'm a big fan of your movies. Could use your help. Thanks. Say hey to your brother, Loki, for me."

Wait, wasn't Loki a troublemaker even if the actor who played him had incredible eyes. "Never mind, don't say anything to Loki." Last thing she needed was someone meddling in her problems. She had enough issues without a troublesome Norse deity sticking his nose in her business. Henry the janitor knocked on her window.

"Morning." He grinned at her displaying his two gold teeth.

She turned off the car, waited for the man to step back before swinging the door open. "Hello, Henry."

"Finish your conversation with your boyfriend. What's his name, Thor?"

No one was immune to gossip in Monrovia. She would have thought the elderly man had no interest in passing along rumors, but it looked as if she was wrong. "Ah, Thor is a pet name. It's a new relationship. He's not exactly my boyfriend."

The man nodded his silvered head. "Got it. Pet names, already, though. What does he call you?"

Her eyebrows went up as she searched for a suitable name. "Freya?" She asked with a definite question in her voice.

"Ah, you do know Thor and Freya were brother and sister?"

"Oops!" She shrugged her shoulders, unaware of how she got caught up in the story. "I better research my mythology before I make any more mistakes."

"You do that." Henry turned to the library door and swung it open for her. She walked through hoping that maybe Thor sent the man to escort her to Leticia. Surely, the woman wouldn't fire her with an audience. She climbed the steps to the reference area as a heavy sense of expectation crouched on her shoulders.

The library overhead lights flickered to life as a cheerful humming penetrated the stacks of books, teasing Darcy and drawing her closer. Leticia Blankenship never hummed. If she did, a funeral dirge might be appropriate. The woman she was seeking drifted into view, humming. Unbelievable.

"Good morning, Darcy." The stern librarian managed a smile.

Oh, my goodness, she was almost nice. "Ah, good morning to you." She wanted to ask if she still had her job, but it would be better to say nothing. She read somewhere about a man who kept reporting to work two years after his firing. Since he kept working, the company kept paying him. Maybe that would work for her. "Do you want me to start with shelving?"

Leticia held up one finger.

Oh, great, here it comes.

"I need you to send notes to everyone whose library card is about to expire."

Darcy nodded, while mentally she cheered, *I still have a job.* "Library notecards?"

"Of course."

"I'm on it."

"One more thing." She gave Darcy's outfit a considering look. "Glad to see you're more appropriately dressed today. I was going to fire you."

Her breath caught in her throat as she focused on the word *was.* Before she could ask about her mind change, Leticia kept talking.

"My nephew talked me out of it. He's a charmer like his father, Sean."

She needed to find out who her nephew was and buy him a beer. He probably had coke bottle glasses and sported a pocket protector. "Is your nephew visiting?"

The woman gave her a sharp look. "He's not for you. Be glad you still have your job. Truthfully, I doubt I could have found anyone else to work for so little, especially part time. You may be a bit odd, but at least you read."

It was probably as close to a compliment as Leticia ever gave her. "Thank you."

"That wasn't a compliment, just a fact."

Talk about a slap down. "I'll get right on those expiring library card notes." Darcy moved toward the circulation desk before she revealed her real feelings with a facial tic or something. Her shift was only four hours long, and she didn't work at Sweaty's tonight. It would be almost a day off. The potential of close to a whole day tempted her as she arranged the notes on the desk. There couldn't be that many expiring cards.

An hour and half later, her right hand was cramping from writing endless renewal notes. She forgot about the second-grade teachers bringing in their classes to get library cards on the same week, which meant the now fourth graders' cards, would expire at the exact same time. No wonder, Leticia passed on firing her today. Only thirty more cards to go.

When the clock hand finally moved to two, she felt like shouting with joy. She carefully tidied her area, stacked the stamped cards, and carried them back to Leticia. The woman looked up from her lunch of tuna fish casserole. "Are you leaving?"

"I can stay until you finish your lunch. I was going to take the cards to the post office."

The librarian waved her free hand. "Leave the notes. I need to check them to make sure you got them all."

"I expected as much. I alphabetized them for easy perusal." She kept her voice even, not wanting Crabby McCrab to know how much her micromanaging actions irritated her.

"Good. At last, you seem to be catching on. Maybe I can mold you into a proper librarian."

Darcy kept her face free of emotions, but it didn't stop her mind from working overtime. *I need to get out of this town, yesterday.* "I'll see you tomorrow."

Leticia stared down at the cards, frowning as she looked through them without bothering to reply. Typical. Often no reply was better than one. At least, she could tiptoe out of the place while she still had a job. Laundry awaited her.

Chapter Seven

OUTSIDE THE LIBRARY, the sun shone, the temps remained in the seventies, but the scent of burning leaves rode the breeze. It was the best time of the year with the muggy, sweltering days of summer in the rearview mirror. Too bad she didn't have anything more exciting to do than hitting the local Laundromat. Her small car waited in the almost empty parking lot. Five cars counting hers, and she knew one belonged to Leticia. Even though she'd spent the five months bending over backward trying to please the difficult librarian, her job could be in danger more from people not using the library.

Plenty of small communities closed their libraries due to former patrons doing their research from the comfort of their own couch via the Internet. William had reminded her more than once that people no longer read and her desire to be a writer wasn't viable. Easy for him to say when whatever he did turned to gold. Even now, he was planning his marriage to a woman who adored him. They'd have perfect, well-behaved children, too.

Her cheer at having a half day off, tumbled as she opened the car door. Her nose wrinkled as she started the car and reversed it. "I'm being petty." Despite her words, it didn't stop her resentment. Her parents always made sure to state they loved both of them equally, but she had her doubts. Why would they even say that, unless they felt like they had to? It was reminiscent of her short-lived romance with Roan.

When she eventually tracked him down, he insisted it wasn't her, it was him. Yeah, right, had anyone ever believed that line?

It didn't help that the man married his second cousin six months later. Maybe she had been the man's one attempt to broaden his family's gene pool. She turned toward her home, one foot in the self-pity camp, while something tickled the edge of her memory.

"My family loves me. It's my observations that bug them. It didn't matter if they were true or not. Just as well, I didn't mention our felonious minister or the missing emeralds. It might be the excuse they needed to send me somewhere for my own health. The retreat would have tall walls, doctors, and padded rooms."

The car shuddered. "Damn it. This is the last thing I need. Rocky, you were supposed to last me until I made it to the big city with public transport."

The car gave another shudder, a long wheeze, as she steered it to the shoulder and stopped. *Did she ask what else could happen?* Her great grandmother had warned her that complaining was tempting the gods to put another obstacle in her path. She'd also warned her that being proud of someone could result in having the person taken away from you since the gods were jealous. Her own mother dismissed the ominous warnings by pointing out that they didn't believe in the Norse deities. True, but what if the same temperamental supernatural beings believed in her.

The radio continued playing, but Darcy switched it off to conserve the battery. The fuel gauge arrow hovered below the red E. Her hand slapped the dashboard. That's what she'd forgotten. Traffic continued passing her. No one stopped. The school buses she could understand, but what about the people pulling campers, boats, or horse trailers. They weren't on the clock.

A large, conservative sedan stopped behind her. Thank goodness, a good guy showed up to save the day. She glanced in her rear-view mirror, recognizing her minister. The absolute last person she wanted to see. Darcy reached for her glasses and pushed them on just in time. There was a tap on her window.

"You need help?"

It might look that way. "No, no, I'm fine." She shouted the words through a closed window. *Go away. Quit trying to be helpful. You don't have to impress me with your helpful ways since I know what you're really like.*

"Are you lost?"

The man didn't give up easily. What excuse could she come up with that he might accept and stop trying to help? If he knew she heard him in the library, he might help her on her way to the pearly gates.

"I'm, ah, praying. Joseph told us to pray all the time." It may not have been Joseph. Had he even been a disciple? Most of her church time involved creating backstories for all the members. Ironic to find out the minister had a major one.

"Sorry to bother you." He walked back to his car, climbed inside, and drove away.

Darcy closed her eyes and heaved a sigh. "Thank goodness." With the car window stuck in the up position and the air conditioning off the car worked as a terrarium keeping all the heat inside. Sweat beaded her upper lip as she contemplated what she should do. It would be a moderately long walk to Clark's Gas & Bait Depot. She'd be over-charged for gas can rental, and then it would be another long walk back. Might as well get started.

Outside the car, a cool breeze dried her sweat, making her sticky as opposed to glistening. The flat shoes she donned to imitate her librarian boss should be practical for walking, but the left one was rubbing a blister on the back of her heel. Monrovia wasn't the biggest town around so the traffic thinned out after the minister left her in peace. All the folks with boats and campers were out of towners buzzing through on their way to their vacation. It would be nice if Ruby came by and picked her up. Her cell phone, she could call someone. How could she have forgotten? Darcy stopped on the gravel, stepping even further from the road to root through her purse. Lipstick, tissue pack, tampon, her cell rested at the bottom.

"Glory, finally." She swiped her phone to open it. The phone icon showed three missed calls. One was William, another definite hope for picking her up. If the minister hadn't showed up and rattled her so much, she would have remembered to call for help. She accessed the keyboard and typed in her brother's number. Nothing. No ring or anything, which forced her to look at the bar symbol. No bars, which meant she was in a dead zone.

She stomped her foot and cursed, frustrated beyond belief. Might as well have a hissy fit alongside the road, especially since there was no one to see her. A rumble of a high-powered car abruptly stopped her fit as she slowly turned to witness the sexy navy Charger convertible pulling onto the shoulder. The car had nothing on the driver, though. Even with the mirrored aviator glasses on, she knew it was Killian from the bar. A rescue from the handsome visitor would be a fitting ending to a miserable day.

"Do you need help, ma'am?"

His inquiry had her looking around for an elderly lady. Nope, just a few scraggly pines, and a house in the distance. He must mean her. Even her mother bristled at the term. Her eyes dropped down to her no nonsense flats and long skirt. Oh, no! She had on her hideous disguise, which made her look like a combination of lunch lady and church matron. Her fingers went up to her face. Her horn-rimmed glasses were still in place. Her fingers lingered on the glasses as she debated whipping them off. Couldn't do much about anything else.

"Ah, yes, I do. My car stopped." She turned and gestured in the direction she came from, expecting to see nothing but a tiny dot of color where her vehicle sat. Unfortunately, she could make out the vehicle quite well. Had she walked so little? It gave her time to slip off her glasses and hide them in the pocket of her baggy cardigan.

"I thought that might be the issue. I could offer you a ride to wherever you're going. Do you know what is wrong with your car?"

"Ah, it may have run out of gas?" She flushed, knowing the words were true. It wasn't the first time she ran out of gas, either. Most people after experiencing such an incident would be more careful. Besides having a delicious stranger in town, she had to juggle avoid being seen by felons, her brother's upcoming wedding and her part in it, and how to exit town pronto. Gas hardly mattered until she didn't have any.

"Easily remedied." He pulled off his sunglasses and gave her an easy smile.

It wasn't the one from sports bar that had oozed promise. Nope, this was the congenial expression reserved for teachers, parents, and lost children. "I could drive you where you need to go, but me being a stranger I'd understand you not wanting to…"

Before he could finish his sentence, Darcy swung the passenger door open and slid onto the leather seat. Sure, she'd have liked to meet under different circumstances, but a ride was a ride. Another hundred yards and she'd accepted a ride from Ronny even though it might confirm the gossip that the two of them were knocking boots.

Killian's eyebrows beetled together as he shoved his sunglasses back on. "Where to?"

His strong chin and muscular shoulders prompted a few possibilities she didn't even dare mention, especially in her current outfit. Never mind seducing a man when she looked like an escapee from the nursing home. It would be hard to flirt. The man would probably wreck the car if he thought she was making a move on him. Darcy needed to add a little oomph to her outfit.

"Ah, it's hot." She wiggled out of her oversized sweater, exposing the prim buttoned to the throat blouse. There was no delicate way she could casually unbutton it. Maybe when he looked away to drive, she'd do it. Men had a radar for any skin display below the collarbone. He'd notice.

"Safety first," Killian announced as he flipped on his blinker.

What was he talking about? Did he want her to applaud his use of a turn signal? Sure, it could be a rarity in these parts since everyone pretty much knew where they were going and figured everyone else did too. They usually did. Only out of towners or a law enforcement would be concerned with traffic rules. Her eyes narrowed as she considered the latter. "What are you in town for?" He lacked the overconfident swagger of her previous beau. Clyde, the cook, labeled bully with a gun. Initially, she resented the summation until she discovered how true it was.

Killian on the other hand had a sense of humor. She could trust him. The man in question turned and leaned over Darcy making her wonder if she spoke too soon. The snap of the seat belt allowed her held breath to escape.

"Gotta take precautions in a convertible." He gave a short nod, before shifting the car into drive.

For a moment, she thought he was going masterful on her, not that she was against it. She needed a little warning. Her heartbeat slowed down a little as she picked out the hairpins that held up her messy bun. No one could expect her hair to stay in place in a convertible. The car picked up speed, whipping her hair across her face, making it hard to see. Not exactly what she'd planned.

The wide performance tires grabbed the road. "Pretty sweet ride, I wouldn't mind taking the wheel sometime." No woman came between a man and his vehicle. It was foolhardy to even mention such a thing. If a fellow found himself so crazy in lust that he allowed his new squeeze to drive his car or truck, no male in town would ever let him hear the end of it.

"Do you drive stick?" he asked, not even glancing in her direction.

Under the thick cover of her hair, which made her look more like Cousin It from *The Adams Family*, she unbuttoned two buttons on her blouse. "Do I drive a stick?" She made it sound like an insult while she wondered if the riding lawn mower counted as a manual transmission.

"Not many people do anymore. It was hard even getting a stick model. I special ordered it and waited several months."

Obviously, the car meant a lot to him. No surprise there. She could see through the strands of hair that they were reaching the cross street where he need to turn for the gas station. Monrovia wasn't blessed with a lot of business. One filling station, one bank, one emergency medical center that had five beds if you were sick. The only thing they had more than two of was dance studios started by thwarted dancers or former cheerleaders. "Turn right at the intersection."

He downshifted for the turn. "What happened to your hair?"

At least, he'd noticed her, just not in the way she wanted. She ran her fingers through it trying to comb it into some sort of order. At least, she had a tie on her wrist to lasso her hair into a messy ponytail. "Is that any better?"

"I wasn't complaining. It's just that you got into the car all prim and proper. You lost the glasses, then the sweater."

Her face heated as he catalogued each change. Why did she think it would seem so natural?

The gasoline station came into view, saving her from making intelligent conversation. The usual idle elderly men sat on a bench whiling the day away by commenting on all who visited for gas, a soda, or bait. The throaty roar of the car had them looking up. Unfortunately, she knew every one of them, including Grandpa Willie, who was no blood relative to her, but she'd picked up the habit of calling him Grandpa as did almost everyone under thirty.

She gave a slight wave, knowing it was too much to hope to go unrecognized. Amos tugged at his ball cap, which hid his bald head. He was never a big conversationalist, and she appreciated that. Tuck pushed himself up and walked around the car as Darcy let herself out. The older man approached Killian. "What do you have under the hood?"

Men and their engines, it didn't matter how old they were. She dashed into the small office that served as the mini-mart with a coin operated pop machine and a box of snacks that included a change box for the purchase. A small sign mentioned something about all profits going to the Moose Lodge. The emergency gas can sat in the corner. The owner dressed in grimy overalls stood in the corner, playing an old video game machine that had to be older than she was.

Her fingers wrapped around the can with the plan to get the gas and go, possibly avoiding the ridiculous can rental fee.

"Money first. You know it's five dollars before you pump." He mumbled the words, not even taking his eyes from the game. Probably wiping out aliens to keep the earth safe.

"Clark, you know I'll bring it back."

He grunted with glee as he committed electronic murder. "Yeah, you'll bring it back in about two weeks like you did last time. I had to buy a new gas can."

"Now you have two gas cans. Why get so demanding about one?"

He looked up briefly. "I'm trying to teach you to be better prepared. If the consequences are bad enough you won't go doing the same thing."

She fished a five out of her pocket. No reason to point out she'd just done the same thing again. Talk like that would get the can rental raised to ten dollars, and everyone would blame her. She laid the bill on the video game screen and received a grunt for her actions.

The Monrovia men were charmers. Hard to believe Clark was divorced. She hurried out to the pump before she ended up saying something that would make her even more unpopular if that was even possible. Killian stood by the car while Tuck sat in the driver's seat and pretended to drive. His actions made her smile since the car noises made him sound as if he was five instead of eighty-five.

Before she could even get the gas nozzle into the can, Killian appeared by her side. "Here, let me do it." He wrapped his fingers around the nozzle, touching her fingers. Darcy glanced at their hands crowded together. She almost didn't let go, not because she didn't want Killian to play the gentleman, but it was as close as she'd been to a desirable man in a good, long time.

"Okay." She released the nozzle and stepped back.

Grandpa Willie slid up to Killian and slapped him on the back. "Darcy can pump her own gas. She comes from hardy stock."

Geesh, he made her sound like a cow.

"I don't doubt it." He hung up the nozzle and screwed on the lid. "My mother would have my hide if I didn't help out a woman."

Damn it. That meant he had good manners and wasn't interested in her. "Thank you. You made your momma proud."

He shrugged and grinned. "I try, but my mother has high standards." His car roared to life, causing them both to spin in time to spot a panicked Tuck holding onto the steering wheel with both hands as the car bucked forward about a yard, then stalled out.

Killian handed her the can as he ran to the car. "Are you okay?"

Not exactly what she'd been asking if some old codger messed with her expensive car, which showed her that the man was nice or he could be so rich that he had dozens of cars.

Tuck managed to get out of the car with some help from Amos, who guided him over to the bench. Grandpa Willie waved as he followed his friends to the usual place. He yelled back over his shoulder, "Say Hey to William for me."

"I will." Both she and Killian replied in unison.

"Wait, you don't know my..."

"Get in the car." He took the gas can from her and stowed it on the backseat floor.

She did as he ordered, but decided only this once would she do what he told her to do unless he came up with some excellent suggestions that she wouldn't mind doing.

They pulled out of the parking lot with a honk. The three men waved enthusiastically as if they had met a long lost relative they actually liked. "You certainly charmed them."

"I meant to."

"Why?" She had it on good authority that Grandpa Willie was the one who started the rumor about her saying elves were invading the area. She'd only commented that a few of the festival attendees looked like elves, which was an entirely different matter.

"I was trying to protect your reputation. It would be one thing to be seen with a stranger, but a different matter if your brother's friend helped you out."

"Yeah, you're right." She didn't add that her reputation consisted of her being the local nut job. Some women thought she was insane because she wouldn't give Ronny the time of day. A few may have even contributed fodder for the gossip in hopes that Ronny would give up on her and go after someone else. "What did your new best friends say?"

He shifted into a higher gear, as the approached the highway. "Not a whole lot, they just wanted to know about the car. One warned me off. Told me you were Ronny's girl. Told me the fellow had invested a lot of effort in chasing men off."

She slammed her fist into her hand. "I knew it. I suspected as much when he showed up at Sweaty's and glared at every man I waited on. He's there every night I work."

"I told them I was your brother's friend, and Ronny had no worries."

"Thanks, I think." She pulled off her ugly flats and held them up. "Is it the shoes or the granny skirt?"

He shook his head as eased onto the highway. "I almost wouldn't have recognized you. Did you lose a bet?"

"Something like that." No reason to explain her attempt to butter up the most persnickety woman in town. "I don't normally dress like a sexy referee or a grandmother. In normal life, I try for something between the two."

"Sounds interesting. I might have to check out your wardrobe then."

There was nothing too exciting about her clothes. "Oh, they're not that..." she stumbled to a stop when she realized the man might be asking her out. The car slowed as he turned into a cut through to reach the other side of the road where her car sat. "You aren't asking me out are you?"

He coasted to a stop behind her car and switched on the ignition. "That's what I thought I was doing. Maybe I'm doing it wrong. How about it?"

Wow, she couldn't believe it. *Act cool.* She brought one finger up to the side of her face. "I loved to go out with you. I only have one request."

"I'm afraid to ask, but I will. I hope I don't have to wrestle a greased pig."

"Take me somewhere out of town."

He lifted one eyebrow, "Are you trying to avoid Ronny?"

She hoped to avoid everyone else in town who might feel obligated to tell Killian what a space cadet they believed her to be just because she imagined things differently. "What I'm trying to avoid is hanging out at Sweaty's."

"Yeah, I could see how that could be a problem. Is tonight too soon? You'll have to advise me where to go."

Before she could answer, he swung his door open, lifted the gas can out of the back and walked over to her car. He'd have been out of luck if she had a locking gas cap that worked. It might be the reason behind her odd gas consumption, too.

She followed him, knowing she'd have to drive her rattletrap car home that somehow appeared even shabbier after Killian's ride. "Tonight's perfect. Simpsonville has a movie theatre, and there's an Italian restaurant not too far out of town."

He grinned at her over the roof of her car as he emptied the gas can. "Seven sound good to you."

"Sounds wonderful." She reached for the gas can. He pulled out of her reach. "Hey, I need to take that back."

"I'll do it." The empty container went back into his car. "You go on home and burn that outfit or something." He jumped into his ride and roared away.

Darcy stood beside her car staring off in the direction that Killian went. "You don't have my number."

Chapter Eight

DARCY FISHED OUT the date perfume from behind the various discarded toiletries and makeup. The liquid inside the oval bottle looked darker than usual. She held it up to the bathroom light while her teeth sunk into her bottom lip,

"Ruby, does perfume go bad?"

Her rumpled impromptu roommate strolled to the open bathroom door. Rube grabbed the container, sprayed the perfume into the air, and sniffed it. "Ugh. It is supposed to smell like perm solution?"

"No. I don't think so." Last time, she used it was—her eyes rolled up as she tried to remember. Was it that fix up with her brother's friend? It could be her disastrous decision to go out with Ronny, but that was an impulsive move. It hadn't merited the dating perfume. "Ah, I got it down at Lavender's. The sales clerk told me it was very popular."

"Ha, that explains it." Ruby held the bottle up to Darcy's nose. "Take a good whiff. It's a scent guaranteed to keep any amorous man far away. I'm sure it is popular with all the women who have long lost interest in their husbands. It's not the perfume a woman wears if she wants to get laid."

Darcy sniffed the scent, unwilling to spray it and get it on her. Her nose wrinkled at the strong, acrid smell. Why did she buy it is the first place? Oh, yeah, the boutique employee mentioned it would be perfect for her. "It does smell bad. Could be the reason I never had a second date with William's friend. By the way, it's a date, not a booty call."

"Please." She stretched out the word with a grin. "I saw the man. There's not a woman in town who would mind tall, dark, and delicious putting his boots underneath her bed. If you wear that perfume, you might as well put your grandmother outfit back on. Nothing spells desirable like orthopedic hose."

Darcy's reflection grimaced at her from the mirror. Ruby wiggled her eyebrows catching sight of her own image.

"They were knee socks, not hose. You know good and well I was toadying up to my stick up her butt boss. How would I know I'd run out of gas, and Killian would show up to rescue me?"

"Yeah, if anyone else mentioned the same thing. I wouldn't believe them, but they'd also be wearing their daisy duke shorts and a shirt unbuttoned low enough to expose the lace on their pushup bra. No female would be caught dead in your granny librarian outfit. I'm surprised Clark even let you take his can after you held on to the last one."

"Ah yeah, that. He charges a deposit now." Darcy turned sideways and smoothed her hands over her T-shirt dress that had a colorful lizard twining around her. "Do you think this dress strikes the right note between casual and flirty?"

She rocked up on her toes trying to see the hem of her dress in the mirror. Heels would be a necessity to accent her legs. They could be the reason behind the invite since her waitress outfit exposed every inch of her well-proportioned limbs. Ruby made some grumbling noises behind her. "Go ahead and tell me. It's not like you to hold back."

Ruby pointed at her dress. "That would be good if you worked at the zoo as the reptile lady."

"What? I like this dress. Besides, he's taking me out to the Italian place. Jeans might not be enough. I don't exactly have a huge wardrobe to choose from. What do you suggest?"

"Wait here." Her friend's face disappeared from the mirror as high-pitched giggling trailed down the hallway.

"A person would think she was going out with Killian." She addressed the mirror. Her lips twisted to one side. "It's no more ridiculous than me thinking the man would show since he doesn't have my phone number, address, or even my last name. Who am I kidding?" Her shoulders slumped forward just as Ruby returned with a red polka dotted dress.

"See your lizard getup even depressed you. Quick, get changed!" She shoved the dress and strapless bra in her direction. "I bought this for when Ernie and I reached St. Louis. We were planning on painting the town red. That's why I bought a red dress."

The full skirted halter dress tempted her, especially since she'd never wore anything so deliberately sexy. Some people might call her waitress outfit sexy, but those same people would be middle school boys or men that thought like one. There were plenty of them out there. "I'll try it on just because I want to. There's no reason to think I'll be walking out of the door wearing it."

"We'll see." Ruby stepped back into the hall, closing the door behind her. Darcy slipped off her formerly favorite dress. Since she didn't have tons to choose from, it was easy to earn the position. The strapless bra turned out to be a push-up. No big surprise there. The dress material slid over her curves with a cool slither and a sensuous whisper making her feel sexy.

The color warmed her skin. However, her hair needed work. A curling iron, hair oil, and her brush created a sheaf of smooth dark hair slipping over her shoulder. One more swipe of black mascara and a slightly off red lipstick completed her ensemble. All she needed was shoes and earrings.

"Decent?" Her friend trilled before she opened the door and

sprayed something at her.

"Hey!" She held up her hands to prevent another aerosol assault. "What are you doing?"

"Helping out." She handed a pair of chandelier earrings to Darcy. "You look like a movie star. Ah, you know that woman from long ago who had her dress blowing up in the wind."

"Marilyn Monroe." She answered as she fastened the earrings. "She was a blonde and I'm not. She was curvaceous, and I'm not."

"There you go ruining things with facts. At least the dress is the same."

It wasn't, but Darcy chose not to point it out and ruin things with facts. Instead, she inhaled whatever Ruby chose to spritz her with. The top scent note was spicy, rather like chili powder. "You didn't spray me with hot sauce, did you?"

"You'll be hot all right, but no, it wasn't hot sauce. I'm not sure if I should tell you, knowing how you can be."

What was that supposed to mean? A quick, rapid succession of knocks on the front door interrupted anything she might say. Was he here? How could he be? Ruby pushed her out of the doorway toward her bedroom. "Get your shoes on. Keep it sexy. I swear that man candy of yours knocks like a policeman."

"He's not." She asserted before shoving her feet into a pair of strappy sandals. The last thing she needed was a cop. Not only did they think they were God's gift to womankind, you couldn't depend on them. Half the time, they cancelled out claiming work matters. No real way to argue the point or check it out. Yeah, work usually had implants and hung upside down from a pole.

Darcy could hear Ruby talking to Killian, which caused her to rush as much as she could in four-inch heels. Her friend might decide to mention how long it had been since she'd been on a date or hint that she'd be out if the two of them wanted to return and shake the mattress. Although, the idea did have appeal, she hoped for more subtlety.

Her skin flushed as she mentally planned her night. Her heels clicked as she reached the strip of linoleum that served as the foyer.

Killian glanced her way and whistled. "Wow! You're gorgeous."

The compliment flowed over her like warm honey. Unfortunately, like most men, Killian didn't know when to stop talking.

"Did you see that outfit she had on earlier today?"

Ruby nodded her head and giggled.

He held out his hand to Darcy and winked before adding, "My grandmother has more stylish clothes. I thought I was being punked."

Her fingers already rested in his large palm as he finished his teasing remark. Darcy jerked to pull them away, but his fingers wrapped around hers before she could.

"Ah, not so fast. You know, I'm joking. Besides, I've been looking forward to this date since forever."

It sounded like a practiced line to her, but his sincere eyes, breathed some truth into it. "Does a couple hours equate forever?"

His low laughter wrapped around her, making her want to say something else that would make him laugh. "No, just about twenty-four hours since Ruby slipped me your phone number and address at Sweaty's."

Darcy did a double take. Here she thought her friend was making a play for the new guy in town when she really was being a wing woman. "Ruby, why didn't you tell me?" Her friend shrugged, but didn't need to add she'd been too preoccupied with William's engagement. That had been obvious.

Wait a minute, when Killian picked her up, he already had her phone number and address. She transferred her gaze to Killian, which involved looking up even with her heels. "What's your story? You didn't even mention you had my number. You hadn't called me?"

He sighed. "Trust me; I was tempted, especially around midnight when I couldn't get to sleep."

"Aww," Ruby provided background sounds despite Darcy waving her away with her free hand at hip level.

"You can tell me more in the car." She cut her head to the slightly open door and wouldn't have been surprised to see half the building's population standing in the hall. Anyone new was worthy of interest.

"Will do, boss."

He smirked at her, but somehow managed to make it both annoying and endearing. It could be the strong chin line or the dimple that showed up in his left cheek when he smiled.

Darcy gave an airy wave, then clutched Killian's arm. Unlike some women who held onto their guy to demonstrate possession, she just wanted to get down the stairs without twisting an ankle.

Killian wrapped his arm around her waist. "No worries. I won't let you fall. My idea of a fun date doesn't include driving you to the emergency room."

"That's good because it wasn't under my definition, either." His fingers pressed slightly into her waist as they reached the landing.

His navy muscle car glistened in the setting sun attracting admirers. The euphoria she felt walking down the steps beside Killian vanished when she saw a couple of grizzled locals. Oh, they'd want to talk engines, which would delay their date. Monrovian men had a talent for wasting time talking about stuff they already knew. Killian would end up into a long-winded conversation.

"You own this car." The man with a dirty John Deere cap motioned to the vehicle.

"I do." Killian nodded in the man's direction. "Thank you for not leaning on it. I've shined it up to take my special lady out tonight."

John Deere Cap man leaned back to look around her. Even though, he was a neighbor, they'd never really met, except to pass at the dumpster. "Ah, where is she?"

Killian dropped a kiss on Darcy's hair, causing her to close her eyes and savor the moment. How much better could it get?

"Right here." His cupped hand nudged her, forcing her to open her eyes or she'd stumble around as if playing Blind Man's Bluff.

Killian swung the passenger door open and assisted her into the car. Darcy smiled up to him. If this was what men were like outside of Monrovia, then she needed to leave immediately. Well, make that after a certain construction worker left town.

His tall form circled the convertible, allowing her to feast on his sweet body garbed in black pants and a dark striped shirt that had a thin strip of something metallic that glistened when the sun hit it. Her lips pursed as she considered the man. Normally, dark colors usually wouldn't work that well on someone with his coloring, but Killian nailed it. Put a hoop earring in his ear, add a pair of black leather boots and he could serve as a template for a sexy pirate. The thought made her squirm in her seat.

The car door slammed, and Killian reached for his seatbelt. "You ready?"

"Am I." Her enthusiastic response caused her date to do a double take.

"You must be hungry." He grinned in her direction and started the car. The engine came to life.

"You have no idea." She needed to stop her mouth somehow. With any luck, he didn't hear her over the car noise. The rearview mirror reflected the stunned faces of her neighbors. Were they surprised that such a smooth, considerate man visited their town or that he asked her out. Probably the latter.

The scenery flashed by as the car ate up the miles. Her desire to be seen with Killian warred with her desire to get out of town before Ronny heard about her date and made a scene. Since everyone in

Monrovia could call half the population cousin, it meant one of her neighbors was speed dialing to inform Ronny.

"Turn right at the next intersection up here." She flung out her right hand as if he wouldn't know what direction she meant.

The man sped on ignoring her directions. Had she just made a huge mistake? Maybe Killian was working with the felon minister and his convict friend. Several months from now, she'd be featured on one of the tabloid magazine shows with some title like **Women Who Made a Fatal Mistake**. It could have a worse title such as **Horny Women Willing to Jump the First Sexy Stranger Who Came to Town**. Too long, but it would be accurate.

Chapter Nine

VINYL SIDING HOUSES with corrugated metal carports replaced the older brick homes with the long front porches and flower decked lawns. Barns surrounded by white washed fences supplanted the houses. Every now and then a cow, horse, or even a goat would stop grazing long enough to watch them zoom by. Would the last creature to see her have four legs?

Even though she enjoyed reading mysteries, watching the occasional thriller, and could play a good game of Resident Evil, she had no experience in extracting herself from life-threatening situations. The car slowed a little, and Killian glanced at her.

"Why are you gripping the door handle?"

Her knuckles had whitened due to her tight grasp. "I am?" Her fingers loosened as she forced a small chuckle and returned his gaze. Damn, the man was hot. The chiseled features made him resemble an action hero while his dark brown eyes, reminded of her childhood pet, Lucky. Puppy dog eyes or not, most serial killers were cold blooded and ruthless, except for the ones who had some issues with their mother. They were creepier. "How's your mom?"

He blinked before turning his attention back to the road. Oh, great, her imagination ran amuck as it sometimes did and stomped out any hope she might have of a love life.

"Mom's great as usual. Everyone loves my mother. She had a huge heart and a sneaky way of getting her way. You know her?"

He slowed as the fields turned into gently rolling hills with groves of maples, oaks, and the silver birches. There were no restaurants, no shopping malls, or anything else that would motivate Killian to drive this way.

A small brown sign announced a park as Killian flipped on his turn signal. Oh yeah, she'd forgotten there was a park out here. Her sixth-grade trip took place here. "It's a park."

"You're right." He turned into the park and followed the arrows to the waterfall path. "When you suggested you didn't want to see anyone from town, I researched the surrounding area at the library."

Goodness, she hoped he didn't see her stick up her butt boss or worse talk to her. "Ah, the library."

"Yes. There was this older gentleman there who manages this park and suggested a picnic here."

A picnic sounded rather romantic. "It will get dark soon."

"I know. I bought a lantern. We could even look at the stars."

Ooh, even more romantic. "Did you bring a blanket?" Would they sit at those uncomfortable wooden picnic tables and crane their necks at an awkward angle to view the night sky?

"Of course." He pulled the car into a parking spot near a group of pines with a small sign indicating the waterfall was less than a quarter mile hike away. "This isn't my first picnic."

Darcy would bet good money that plenty of women loaded down wicker baskets with fried chicken, potato salad, and homemade chocolate chip cookies if Killian hinted at a picnic. "Ah, what are we going to do about food?"

Never mind that her strappy sandals would make walking practical-ly impossible. Forget the lacy lingerie. It wasn't that she had anything against nature. The green expanse and shadowy trees did not figure into the evening she planned as she went all out on her makeup and even used Ruby's lucky perfume.

"No worries. I talked to Gladys at The Porker Delight Deli, and she put together a nice picnic for us."

Her eyes squeezed shut as she held in a moan. Gladys was Ronny's mother. "Ah, you didn't tell her who you were going out with?"

The car door opened, and Killian stood, stretching his hands over his head. "It wasn't a secret, was it?" His forehead furrowed as he waited for her answer.

"Of course, not." She explained in a rush. "I'm not seeing anyone, but, ah, this is a small town and all." That just made it worse.

Instead of responding, he popped the trunk, pulled a stadium blanket out along with a couple of food bags stamped with a smiling pig. Darcy waited in the car, trying to decide if she'd be better off to go barefoot as opposed to aerating the ground with her narrow heels.

Killian swung the door and held his hand out. "I know right now you're probably cursing me for not telling you to change into something more comfortable, but call me selfish."

She took his hand and allowed him to help her out of the car. His comment puzzled her. "Why are you selfish?"

His laughter tickled her ear as he wrapped his free arm around her and pulled her close. "Ah, you couldn't guess. You looked good enough to eat. Quite a step up from the costume you had on when I picked you up earlier."

Her elbow landed firmly in his ribs before she even considered her actions, which caused him to laugh louder.

"You're the best. Any other woman would call me rude, possibly pout, but not you. That's what I like about you. Your honesty." He turned with his arm still wrapped around Darcy. "I thought we could picnic near the trees."

Not too far, she could probably navigate it barefooted once they stepped off the gravel. "Okay, I'll need to take off my shoes, or I'll end up planting them in the dirt."

His gaze dropped to her feet. "Damn, never considered that." He dropped the food bags inside the convertible, slung the blanket over one shoulder, and then scooped Darcy up into his arms.

"Hey!" She grabbed for his blanket free shoulder. "What are you doing?" Since he was striding across the grass with her in his arms, it appeared to be a no-brainer. Darcy couldn't remember any man carrying her anywhere. An impromptu slide down the hill sprained her ankle at church camp. Her boyfriend at the time, Joey helped her limp to the nurse's office, but he even complained about that.

"Problem solving." He bounced her into the air, making her squeal before he caught her.

She pounded him on the shoulder. "Why did you do that?"

"You were supposed to hold on to me tighter, not beat on me."

"Hmm. Does that work with all the other women?"

"Hard to say since you're the only one I carried so far except for work."

Darcy beamed, glad he hadn't been toting any other women around. She'd driven past more than one construction site where not once were the burly construction workers toting women around. "Why would women need to be toted around on the construction site?"

"Well, ah."

KILLIAN HESITATED, KNOWING he'd put his foot in it. He didn't want anyone to know he was a cop or the reason he was in Monrovia. The best lie was the one closest to the truth.

"Ah, the woman fell and hurt herself. I carried her out." It sounded better than mentioning the woman got caught in the crossfire.

"Oh." Darcy's eyebrows went together, expressing her puzzlement. "I guess construction sites can be dangerous."

"They can." No need to mention he hadn't been at a site. They'd reach the spot he had decided on for a picnic. "We're here." He dropped a kiss on her hair as he put her down. "I'll get the food."

He strode back to the car, unwilling for her to see the effect she had on him. A smart girl like her would know. The dozen steps or so were enough to give himself a self-talk. Two Killians wrestled for control. The burned version warned him that no good would come from interacting with a small-town girl. *Watch out, buddy. This is not a good time.*

The other voice he felt represented who he used to be before his partner was gunned down. *Darcy is sexy, funny, and honest. What is there not to like? If they only had a fling, what could it hurt? It might even turn into something more.*

He reached the car without coming to any type of conclusion of how the evening should unwind. From the moment, he dropped her at her car today, his emotions shifted about every five minutes. No wonder he was at a park in the only pair of dress pants he packed. His initial decision was to take her to the fancy Italian restaurant Darcy suggested. The cynical Killian suggested the park after he'd got into the car. At least that way, it wouldn't seem too much like a date, just hanging out really. Make that hanging out with food. Despite, what he implied he hadn't said anything to Gladys despite her nosy questions.

People gossiped in cities, too. He would barely be out of The Porker Delight Deli parking lot before gossip had made Killian and Darcy into an item. He didn't plan on being in Monrovia more than a month and less if called back earlier. No good would come out of making a big deal of a date. It would only embarrass Darcy when he left, although it felt rather high schoolish bringing a girl out to the park with night coming on. He might as well have asked her if she wanted to watch the submarine races, which always served as make out code.

By the time, he'd retrieved the food and lantern, Darcy had

smoothed out the blanket and reclined on her side with her head propped on her hand and a come hither smile on her face.

Seriously. If his hands weren't full, he might have covered his eyes. He had almost ninety percent convinced himself to drive her straight back after eating. His plan was to not touch her, at least not any more than he had. Parts of him weren't on board with his plan, but it was still the right thing to do.

He closed his eyes and inhaled. The seductive scent of her perfume wafted on the breeze. "Are you all right?"

His eyes opened to find her sitting up with a concerned expression.

"How could I not be since I'm here with you, on a warm evening surrounded by all this…" He used the hand with the lantern to gesture to the trees. "…natural beauty."

"Sounds like something a character in a romcom movie might say."

"Oh, really." He placed the food on the blanket as he knelt beside it. "Are you accusing me of appropriating lines from a movie?" His tone was gruffer than he intended. Had he always been like this? If so, it explained why he ended up with women like Heather who had no real interest in him except how she could use him.

"No." Her shoulders shrugged. "Never heard any male from Monrovia be so poetic."

Poetic wasn't much better than stealing lines from movies.

A slow smile lit up her face as she declared, "I like it."

He scooted closer, trying to come up with something else somewhat lyrical. It would be a challenge since most of the time he hardly spoke. When he did, it might be trash talk with another officer or converse with his mother, who had set him up on yet another unasked for date. *Could his mother have planned his meeting with Darcy?* His chin moved side to side as considered the possibility. His mother did suggest heading out to his aunt's to wait for things to cool down. He thought the idea was to help the aunt out, not fix him up.

He shook off the thought.

"Bug in your ear?"

"What?"

"You shook your head as if you have a bug in your ear."

If he kept getting lost in his own thoughts, he wouldn't have to worry about discouraging any real interest. Darcy would mark him down as weird. "It was a bug. It's gone now. Let's eat."

He opened the bags and brought out fried chicken, deviled eggs, pasta salad, and brownies. The second bag contained a bottle of wine and a sleeve of plastic wine glasses.

"Pretty impressive." Darcy peeked into each container. "Brownies." She giggled, batted her eyes, and shook a finger at him. "Ruby told you, didn't she?"

"Told me what?" He couldn't really remember Ruby saying much beside this is her number.

"I love brownies. You won me with the brownies."

He grinned as he pulled out a screw top bottle of bargain wine. "This was all I could get at the deli. They didn't have any corkscrews, either."

Darcy reached for the bottle and pulled it closer to read the label. "I remember this. Had it at my prom. As for the corkscrew, locals don't like to be slowed down in their consumption of alcohol. Most can pop open a bottle of beer with a table edge. The other half is Bible club regulars, which means they buy their spirits in the next county."

His eyebrows lifted as an acknowledgment to her observation skills. "You know this how?"

She pulled the paper plates out of the bag and placed two on the blanket. "Ah, you think I never get out of town. I went up to Lyndon with my mother who gets her hair done up there. She doesn't want anyone to know she's not a natural blonde. Anyhow, we go out to eat at this little bar and grill near the salon. We walked through the bar to the restaurant. Sitting in the bar sucking down margaritas was our pastor's wife. She didn't see us"

"I take it you didn't say anything."

"Of course not." She ladled out pasta salad onto the plates. "At the time, I figured she had her reasons Now, I understand more."

"People would disapprove of a minister's spouse who tippled." He snapped together the plastic wine glasses that appeared none too sturdy. "We lucked out on the wine glasses since they are left over from New Year's." He turned the glasses displaying the logo *Happy 2014.*

"The locals aren't big on wine glasses, plastic or otherwise. Monrovia is a beer drinking region. If you order wine, you get your choice of red or white served in a juice glass."

"Fancy. You like it here?" He wasn't sure if he hadn't asked her this question previously. Small talk wasn't something he did.

She shot him a disbelieving look. "Does it sound like I like it here?"

That would be a no. "Here, have some wine." He offered her a filled glass. "Wait until I fill mine and we can toast." That left him less than five seconds to think of something witty.

Darcy held her glass aloft. "I have one. Here's to getting busy."

His mouth dropped open. Damn, he liked this woman.

She cleared her throat. "I mean, getting busy with the food." Her nose crinkled. "Ugh. That's worse. Let's eat and accept I'm no good at toasts."

His glass tapped hers lightly. "No worries. I couldn't come up with anything either. If I could I would have said something about being adrift in your magnificent eyes."

"Aww. That works." She leaned forward and brushed a kiss against his cheek. He turned his head slightly, allowing their lips to meet briefly. Just as sweet and tender as he expected her lips to be. He paused and tossed back the glass of wine. Darcy gulped her wine and gave him sultry smile.

"You hungry?"

"Not for food." She pushed both their plates off the blanket and removed the food bags.

He recognized the look in her eyes since it had to be a reflection of his own. No reason for him to act like a hormone-driven teenager. He knew better. Yeah, but sometimes knowing better didn't equate doing better. "You sure?"

Chapter Ten

WAS SHE SURE? Killian played the part of the gentleman, allowing her time to refuse. "I think I've been waiting for this since I saw you outside the library."

"I've waited longer."

"How's that. I only saw you the other day,"

He stood holding out his hand and helped her up. "I thought we might try for something more private. As a former boy scout, I know enough to keep us out of the poison ivy."

"Good, because I was a lousy girl scout." She slipped off her sandals, willing to forgo some twigs and pebbles for sex in the woods with an enticing stranger. Geesh, it sounded like the title to a tell-all article in some confessions magazine. Maybe she could write about it and get the money she needed to leave town. With any luck, she could accomplish it before felon minister and pal put an abrupt end to her plans.

Killian lifted up a low hanging branch and held out his other hand for her. They tangled their fingers together and silently moved down the shadowy path. Her breath sounded loud in her ears. This wasn't who she usually was, but it *could be* who she was tonight.

"There's a spot over there under that one tree, and it's close to the stream."

The pine needles under her feet cushioned them as opposed to poking them. The water rushing over the rocks made a comforting sound. Above them some of the birds called out to one another as they settled down for the night. Killian knelt to smooth out the blanket. His black pants stretched over a truly noteworthy ass.

"Why are you dressed up for a picnic?"

"I decided on the picnic at the last minute. He stretched out on the blanket and motioned her closer.

It explained the clothes, but not the mind change. Still, with the man stretched out like a provocative advertisement, it made it hard to stay on topic. "Why'd you change your mind?"

He locked the hands behind his head. "I wanted you to myself. Sure, the restaurant would be nice. We might stumble across your boozing pastor's wife."

Darcy dropped to her knees and crawled closer to Killian. "I didn't say she was boozing." Why they were talking about other people made no sense. "I realize things are hard in a small town with everyone in your business."

"Come here." He rolled onto his side with his arm up. She snuggled into the space with her back to his chest. Maybe she should have turned the other way. His arm wrapped around her waist and pulled her snug against his body. This was good.

They laid in a warm, companionable silence. Darcy closed her eyes. *What a change to be with something who wasn't all hands. A man, not a boy.* Contentment swam through her veins, making everything soft and romantic.

"You happy?" He purred the question into her hair.

"Very." She rolled in his embrace to see his face. "You're looking pretty smug with yourself."

"As I should." He waggled his eyebrows and then kissed her nose. "Consider that I'm here with you. My life suddenly got better." His hand smoothed her hair away from her face.

"Nothing would make it better?" She slid one leg over his. "Too bad, I some ideas." She gave an exaggerated sigh. "I wouldn't want to ruin the moment."

"I'm open to suggestions." His hand slid down her body to cup her derriere. "Tell me."

Now was the time to suggest something sexy. Mercy, she may have started something she couldn't finish. Improvise. "We could play strip poker."

"Sounds intriguing, but don't you need cards?"

He had a point. *Think vixen.* "Amateurs need cards. Tell me what you have and I'll tell you my cards."

His husky laughter rumbled his chest. "I'm already liking this game. I have two threes, a queen of hearts, and a ten of spades. And you?"

"Three kings and two tens. You lose. The shirt goes." She gave an encouraging nod.

"All right. You'll have to help me since there is no room to stand."

"Glad to." Her fingers went to his shirt with the intention of unbuttoning them, but they stilled on his shirt.

"What's wrong?"

Darcy's teeth sunk into her bottom lip. No way, she'd admit in most of her romantic encounters either the man pulled a T-shirt over his head or didn't bother to take it off. Killian was an entirely different class. "Nothing. I was prolonging the experience. I've been imagining you with your shirt off. Now, it's happening." She unbuttoned the first button spreading open the shirt as she went. A V of curly dark chest hair appeared. Not a waxer, she kinda expected the hair. It made him more real.

Her fingers moved over his sculpted pecs and flat abs. "You work out?"

"Have to. It comes with the job."

"Oh, I would have thought hauling around timber would have been work enough." She admired the line of hair that led down to his belt buckle. His muscles flexed and tightened as he pushed into a seated position.

"Ah, well, it works different muscles. Can you pull off one sleeve, then I can get the rest of the shirt off?"

Darcy wasn't sure why he couldn't get his shirt off, but didn't mind helping. The shirt slipped off, exposing his back. The expanse of skin tempted her into pressing her cheek against it. "You have a great back."

"People are always telling me that. It's a daily thing."

She laughed as she was supposed to. "They would if you walked around shirtless." A dark tattoo on his left shoulder intrigued her. The vanishing light made it hard to see. "What's your tattoo?"

A quick twist had Darcy pinned to the blanket with Killian looming over her. "I believe this is my hand."

"Not until you tell me what the tattoo is?"

He groaned. "Damn woman, you play dirty. It's three clover leaves strung together. I got it when I was young and stupid. Did a lot of crazy things then."

Her fingers were already under her dress trying to subtly remove her thong as a contribution to what she knew would be a losing hand of imaginary strip poker. "What other crazy things?"

"You may find this hard to believe, but for a short time I was in this all male strip review."

She wiggled, trying to get the thong down her legs, but ended up bumping against Killian's erection. "I'd paid money to see you. Full monty?"

"Some did. I wanted to leave the ladies with some mystery."

"Then, I do feel privileged." She managed to get the thong to her ankles where she kicked it free.

"What did you just fling?"

The man must have eyes like a hawk. "Panties. They were getting hot." She waited a few seconds before she added, "And wet."

His hand slipped under her dress to caress her bare bottom. Darcy squirmed under his hand. Normally, this was when the alarm clock rang, and she woke up. A sudden roll had her on top and both his hands under her dress cupping her ass.

"Let's forget poker." He arched up the rough texture of his pants rubbing against her clitoris. She wiggled slightly enjoying the sensation while searching for a seductive reply. A screech rent the air.

"What are you doing with my woman?"

Just as she feared. Someone had alerted Ronny to her big date, but how in the world did he find her. "Go away, this isn't your business."

The man stomped up to their romantic alcove and shined a flashlight on them blinding them and causing Killian to curse. He placed his hands on her waist and moved her to the side. "I'll handle this."

He jumped into a standing position and confronted Ronny. "Were you following us?"

Good question, she wondered how he managed to find them.

"Didn't need to. You told my mother you were going on a picnic when you bought all the picnic food. I knew what you were up to when Dwayne called me and told me he saw the two of you together."

"Shove off, buddy. Obviously, the lady picked me."

The shorter Ronny wasn't intimidated by Killian's muscular chest. Didn't work as a distraction as it did for her. She grabbed his shirt, felt around for the thong without any luck, and ducked under the tree. Darcy threw the shirt at Killian and skirted around him as Ronny ranted.

"Of course, she picked you. You're a foreigner, exotic with your fast car and expensive haircut. A poor simple girl would be defenseless against you. After you leave town, where will Darcy be?"

She didn't stay to hear the answer, hoping it would be, *not here.* Anything, Killian might say could sour the night even more than it already was. Her bare feet protested the jog up the path. No longer were pine needles soft and accommodating, but took every opportunity to prick her unprotected toes. A pair of raccoons munched on their dinner while a third held up the wine bottle to peer inside. At least someone enjoyed it.

Her strappy sandals were still there. Probably didn't fit any of the wildlife. The real issue was how would she get home?

Could she swallow her total humiliation and ride home with Killian? Ronny's monster truck sat beside Killian's car. As upset as he was, she was surprised Ronny hadn't driven over the sports car. If she let Ronny drive her home, then he'd assume she finally caved to his charms. A familiar automotive rattle sounded before her car rounded the curve with Ruby at the wheel.

She owed the woman big.

Chapter Eleven

RUBY ROLLED TO a stop and swung the car door open. "Was there any blood?"

Darcy glanced over a shoulder in the directions of the woods. No sign of the men, she didn't even want to think of what they might be doing. A few body blows would be the least of her troubles. If they decided to talk might be the real issue. What would Ronny say beside he had dibs on her?

She slid into the passenger seat before answering. "None I saw. If there was, I'd be the one bloodying Ronny's nose. Why in the world did he show up at the wrong time?"

"Hmm." Ruby reversed the car, before continuing her thought. "Define wrong time."

"Let's just say, I owe you a new thong."

"Aw, don't worry about it. You didn't think I'd want used underwear back. Besides, I bought it for Ernie. I wouldn't feel right wearing it for anyone else. Ya' know what I mean."

Actually, she didn't. Still, it would have been awkward returning lingerie that Killian had peeled off her. Too bad, he never had the opportunity. Now, it looked as if he never would. "Sure."

"So, is his package as impressive as the rest of him?" Ruby pulled her lips into a suggestive circle and wiggled her eyebrows.

"I wish I knew." The memory of his muscular chest made her sigh with regret. "Only got his shirt off before Ronny had to come and ruin everything. What is wrong with that guy?"

"Oh, you mean besides him being crazy in love with you."

Darcy shook her head violently side to side. "Please. Who told you that?"

The car emitted a grinding noise when Ruby missed drive and shifted it in neutral. Instead of changing gears, she hit the gas causing the engine to race. The noise made Darcy shudder and poke Ruby.

"Come on, shift the car into drive. It has to hold up long enough for me to get into a big enough city with public transport."

Ruby sucked in her lips, and managed to get the car into the right gear. They passed several cars coming in as they exited the parking lot. "Looks like the locals arrived to defend your honor."

Darcy peered into the vehicles in the twilight, in particular at the good ol' boys that hung out and gossiped. She'd had no clue they went on information gathering trips. "They came for the show. To think they talk about women spreading rumors. What if," she twisted backwards to look at the vehicles, "they jump Killian? Maybe, I should go back and help him. At least, I know the men."

Ruby snorted. "Since you left, Killian and Ronny will both be telling each other that women make no sense. They'll probably have a beer together. Even if they did exchange punches, they'd still go out and have a beer together, and yet we females get the confusing gender label. When women hate you, it doesn't change depending on the circumstances."

"Ah, I guess you're right." Too concerned about Killian, Darcy wasn't really sure since she only half paid attention to whatever Ruby said. "You think he'll be okay?"

"Please. This isn't some drive-in movie where the stranger comes to town is set upon by the locals and then eaten."

"Yuck! Do I even want to know what type of movies you watch?"

She was sure that wouldn't happen. Then again, her money would have been on Ronny not showing up at an inopportune time too.

"No one watches those movies really It's just background noise and an excuse for getting busy."

"Whatever. How can I know if Killian will be okay?"

Making out in the park may not have been up there as a sophisticated date, but she hadn't been exactly unwilling. Her mother would have pointed out that men don't buy the cow when they get the milk free. Of course, in Monrovia, if they got the cow with calf, they ended up married.

"I made a call to Lynette who's had her eye on Ronny for a long time before I even got into the car."

Lynette's over the top actions made Darcy wrinkle her nose since it was no secret about her feelings. The woman had a T-shirt made up that announced she was **Ronny's Girl**. Darcy had assumed that meant Ronny had moved on. He hadn't. He made up his own shirt that read **Lynette is not my girl**. A person would think the humiliation would be enough to cool the woman's ardor, but apparently not. "How will this help?"

"Lynette will track Ronny down and stick to him like a hungry tick since she thinks you're out of the picture. You're out, right?"

Her friend glanced from the road the same time an oversized tractor topped the hill. "Eyes on road. Besides, I was never in the picture. So how is Lynette sticking to Ronny going to let me know about Killian?"

"You know Ronny, and he won't be together since Lynette will be too busy in the comfort mode. After all, she'll see it as her chance to get her foot in the door."

"I'm not so sure she'll call you right back if all that comforting is going on."

"She'll text. After all, we're cousins."

"Of course."

"She refers to you and me being friends as me consorting with the enemy. You know because of you and her beloved."

Darcy didn't even try to fight the eye roll. "You know there is nothing with me and her beloved."

"I know this, but it is hard for her to accept. She sees him as everything she ever wanted in a man."

Darcy made a gagging sound.

"Come on, have you ever taken a good look at what Monrovia has to offer in the single men department? Ronny looks good in comparison. Your brother was at the top of the list." Ruby's voice thinned out into a whine.

"Don't cry. You never had to live with William. He can be a jerk at times. When my mother finally broke down and bought me a bra, he and his friends put it on the dress dummy and practiced removing it. Half the teenage boys in Monrovia had their hands on my bra before I even got to wear it."

Instead of sharing her outrage, Ruby laughed. "I remember that now. Dylan told everyone what it looked like, that it had a rosebud between the cups, and it was a 30 AAA. Didn't even know they made them that small."

Whoa, she had no clue her bra size had been leaked to the public. Just as well, it would have mortified her even more. "I've moved up a few cup sizes since then. I must leave town, especially after this latest humiliation. Outside of hooking up with a senior citizen bike group, do you have any suggestions?"

"You'd think I would as many times as I've left town. Right now, my car is on the fritz, which is why I drove yours. Who knows my car could be rebelling after its abandonment. I used a man for my escape. Somehow, I could pretend it wasn't me doing the leaving, but the man who did, and I only tagged along. Now, people are calling me the

Black Widow since Ernie died."

"Well, you know…"

Ruby held up her hand to stop whatever she might say. "He wasn't the first one to die on me."

"What?" The possibility of her friend killing off another elderly gentleman distracted Darcy from her own issue. "Who? Was it anyone I know?"

"You remember the band director from school?"

"Ol' Megaphone?" He used to stand on a ladder and yell through a megaphone to be heard over the brass instruments.

"Actually, his name was Clint. He was my first." A sniff sounded in the dark car.

"Your first, um, man." It was hard to wrap her head around that the balding fortyish man with a potbelly would have been the one to break Ruby's cherry, especially when she could have had any boy at school. "Or was he the first man who died on you?"

"Both." A small sob escaped with the acknowledgement.

"That explains a great deal. People thought he had a heart attack on the football field after he wandered out there at night anticipating the battle of the bands contest."

"He anticipated, but not the band battle. I never knew he had a bad heart. I fastened his pants so no one knew. I took off and hid at granny's house until I felt able to come back to school and face everyone. Here I thought everyone knew I'd killed Clint, but they didn't. Instead, the rumor was I went into the city for an abortion. Even when you don't do something you still get the label."

A range of emotions shifted through Darcy with her friend's story from surprise to revulsion. "I hear ya. You may be Black Widow, which is kind of 1940's movie glamorous while I'm that crazy chick who makes things up. Just the other day, when I was in the library I heard two men talking about a robbery they committed."

"Everyone knows Henry took the box of bacon from the IGA. Imogene was going to fire him, but decided she couldn't dock his salary if he wasn't working."

"I wasn't talking about Henry." A motorcycle flew past them, causing them both to look.

"Lynette," they said in unison.

Ruby slapped the steering wheel. "I have to admire the woman. A bike would fit inside Ronny's truck bed, and they could ride together in the front. Smart."

"Determined is more like it."

"The heart wants what the heart wants."

Darcy had heard the expression to explain several bizarre couples. "What does your heart want?"

"No. Don't go there. Don't be cruel."

It wasn't hard to figure out what thought preoccupied her friend. "William is just a guy, not too bad, but not extraordinary, either. What you need is a different setting, somewhere people see you for the sweet person you are as opposed to the trashy image they concocted." Personally, the same sentiment could apply to her, though not necessarily the trashy part.

"Who says I have a trashy image?' Indignation made her voice loud in the small car.

"Um, Ruby, you did."

"Yeah, you're right. I guess that's why I'm attracted to these provocative strangers that pass-through Monrovia."

Stranger she'd agreed with, but the P word Ruby was looking for may have been something else rather than provocative. Killian, on the other hand, embodied the word, but she needed to forget about him. All the weirdness so often associated with herself exploded all over him tonight.

It would be hard going to work tomorrow. Everyone would give her the eye. A few would smirk. Already, she had issues with slapping away groping hands at Sweaty's. The new rumor would have the same randy bastards holding onto her butt cheek for dear life, assuming their persistence would be rewarded. It would never occur to them that they had none of the same traits as Killian.

"What are you going to do when your guy calls?"

"Who?"

"You know. Tall, dark, and delicious."

"He won't call. If he does, it will only be to yell at me for putting him in the middle of the screwball farce my life has become. If he took me to the Italian restaurant this wouldn't have happened. No way would we be playing imaginary strip poker."

"Uh. Imaginary what?"

"Never mind."

"Why didn't he?"

"Told me he wanted to be private."

"Uh huh."

"I thought that was sweet at first. You know even when you drive out of the town and go elsewhere, you run into a half dozen people trying to do the same. You remember I told you about the time when my family went to the Italian restaurant and Miss Carmichael, the high school English teacher, was there dressed in a tight gold tube dress. William and I wanted to see who she was with. Dad decided we'd better off going to the root beer stand."

"There is that."

"I told him I didn't want to go anywhere in town because people would always be in our face just like they were. By the time, we reached his car there were at least four men around the car worshipping it."

"Men love their cars."

"Still, none of it makes sense. If he didn't want to be seen with me, why tell the gawkers at the car we were going out?"

Ruby shrugged.

"It doesn't matter. I don't want to see him again."

The car jerked as Ruby slammed on the brakes.

Darcy put out her hand to prevent slamming the dashboard. "What was that for?"

"Ha. I expected the car to be hit by lightning for that bald face lie." The car started moving once her friend decided she had made her point.

"Ha, ha. It doesn't matter. Nothing will come of it. The best thing I can do is hit the road. I keep saying I'm going to, but I never do, claiming I need money. I'm never going to make any at the piss ant jobs I have. Why don't we both head to the city, get a crappy apartment together. There's bound to be jobs. Better than ones, they have here."

"Aw, I don't know." Ruby's brow furrowed.

"What's holding you here?" Her friend never had any issues, leaving before, even if her breaks from the town were short lived. "Don't say what I think you're going to say. That boat has sailed."

"You don't want me to mention Ernie's will and the fact I need to be where I told his lawyer I would be."

If Ruby expected to get anything, then she was an even bigger fool than local gossip mentioned. "You gave him your phone number. Your phone will go with you. It's not like the lawyer is going to drive here. Besides, these things take time. Sometimes, months, even years, depending on how hard his kids will fight you. It would be on the principle as opposed to them wanting any trinket he might send your way."

The man probably forgotten to take his medicine while overwhelmed by her friend's attention. The last thing on his mind would have been changing his will.

Chapter Twelve

D ARCY'S MOUTH HUNG open for a few seconds, before she snapped it closed. At least, Ruby had a practical thought as opposed to moaning about the one who got away. She could make common sense decisions, too. Right now, leaving appeared like the better choice before emerald thieves-r-us decided she may have overheard them. Her clever use of disguise must have tricked them. No one came by the library when she wore her own version of Head Librarian mini-me disguise. The only person who got the benefit of it besides her boss was Killian.

Maybe she could wear it tomorrow if she were still here. "Ah, Ruby. You didn't really burn that outfit I had on earlier, did you?"

"No. There's an ordinance about burning things except for a fire pit. Neither one of us owns a fire pit."

"Good. I may need it."

Ruby grumbled something under her breath as she pulled into the apartment parking lot. All the slots near the apartment were full. Someone must be having a party. She wouldn't miss never being able to park by her apartment, although she couldn't guarantee things would be different elsewhere. "What did you say?"

"You're too pretty to wear that godawful costume."

"Thanks, but I have my reasons. I should wash it."

"Washing won't help."

The cryptic statement made her wonder, but she chose not to ask. The easy answer to all her problems would be to vanish into another city. Even a short break might help. Whenever she and her brother were together anywhere, people would inevitably reminisce about the Halloween costumes her mother made for them, including the bowling pin and ball combo. As the taller twin, William got to be the somewhat less ridiculous pin. If her mother wanted to downplay her baby fat issue, then putting her in a ball costume did her no favors. Unfortunately, the unflattering costume was hard to move around in. She stumbled and rolled down the small hill in their neighborhood. She knocked down four toddlers and traumatized a toy poodle.

As stories went, that wasn't the worst one people could tell. By this time, Killian could be sitting in a booth at Sweaty's having the locals resurrect various stories about her. Now, that helicopter with a search light that was looking for the escaped lion from the feline sanctuary could have been a UFO. Surely, she wasn't the only one who called the sheriff, but the way the locals told it didn't reflect well on her.

They both exited the car caught up in their own musings. Ruby spoke first. "You know the lawyer has my phone number. It's not like he's going to drive to Monrovia. Truth is I don't expect much. Ernie's kids are a bunch of mean spirited brats that are all older than me. Accused me of killing their father. As if too much happiness could do that. Maybe we could try moving to the city. There's nothing to keep us here."

"Yeah, you got that right." Her phone rang, resulting in her digging through her purse as they mounted the steps. By the time, she found it, the ringing stopped. A strange number identified the caller. "Not sure who it was."

"It could have been Killian calling to apologize."

The thought cheered her a little until she realized the man had nothing to apologize for. He didn't cause Ronny to follow them. Of course, if the two of them had managed to stay fully dressed it would have been a trifle less embarrassing. Well, at least they hadn't progressed to the deed. "He has nothing to be sorry for, unless it's asking me out. In that case, I should be the one apologizing. Ruby, I'll never get laid in this town."

She expected laughter to greet her remark. Instead, her friend nodded her head in agreement. "Yep. You got that right. Ronny is a decent guy. He inherited all his father's farm equipment and helps during harvest time. Doesn't even charge anyone. No one would cross him knowing how he feels about you. Everyone figures you'll eventually hook up."

"Everyone?" She placed one hand on her hip, directing a disbelieving look Ruby's way as her bare foot landed on something sharp. "Ouch!" She hopped around on one foot trying to see what pierced her foot.

"You might have stepped on a nail or something. Something none too clean I suspect. Maybe you should swab your foot with bleach. Wait," Ruby slapped her forehead. "I used up all the bleach."

"Ah, should I ask?" The way her night was going the answer couldn't be good.

"Not really. You wouldn't like the answer." Instead of using the key, Ruby rattled the door handle vigorously until the door popped open.

"What did you just do?"

"Opened the door. I lost the key the first time you gave it to me. Your neighbor explained to me how to open your door."

"That settles it. I'm moving tomorrow." It explained the disappearing food, too. Often when she thought she had bread, milk, or cereal, she had none. The phone chimed again, but this number was different. Maybe it could be the agent who requested the first chapter of her novel.

"Hello."

"Don't hang up!" Killian's voice flowed through the phone, into her ear, and sunk down deep where she'd hoped other parts of him would settle before the night ended.

"I'm not hanging up."

Ruby flipped on the living room light, illuminating Sylvester, the cat, on the table eating the cheese off a pizza. Great, that meant smelly cat farts all night.

"Whoa. I don't know what to say. The night didn't turn out like I expected. It started well."

"I agree."

Ruby mouthed the words, *Ask him where he's at.*

"Where are you?"

"I'm outside of Sweaty's walking to my car."

"Sweaty's, huh?" Her friend managed a knowing nod. "I was worried about you. Afraid you and Ronny might get in a fight or something."

The man had the nerve to laugh. "I bet the two of you broke out a six-pack.

"Not at first, no. You and me together finally convinced Ronny that maybe you two wouldn't live happily ever after. Then this chick comes tearing up on a bike, and Ronny has an idea."

This sounded more like one of her stories. She muted the phone against her shirt and spoke to Ruby. "Lynette shows up, and Ronny has an idea."

Her friend gave dramatic shudder.

"Should I ask?"

"Figured you would. I wanted to make sure you heard the story from me before anyone else. Ronny asked me to drive his truck, and he'd drive my car. We'd meet at Sweaty's then exchange keys. We ran to the vehicles before the chick got too close and took off."

"Ronny, let you drive his truck?"

Ruby splayed a hand over her heart and staggered backwards.

"Damn, that man must have worked some magic."

"You let Ronny drive your car?" If she knew he was allowing anyone to drive his car, she should have asked.

"Figured I owed him stealing his girl and his happily ever after in one fell swoop."

Amusement colored his words. Was he amused that she was Ronny's happily ever after? "What happened when you met at Sweaty's?"

"Yeah, that part I wanted to explain."

Here it comes. Everyone warned him away from her, probably saying she needed a keeper or something equally bad. "Go ahead." She pushed her shoulders back and tightened her muscles. It wasn't like she couldn't take it.

"The woman on the bike thought I was Ronny. When I opened the truck door, she was all over me. Kissing and tugging at my clothes. Well, it was a bit embarrassing."

"So, when did she get a clue?" Personally, she felt Lynette knew all along. Killian was taller, more muscular, and better looking.

"It was probably when Ronny started laughing. She called him a bastard, tried to kick him in the nuts, but he managed to sidestep that. She jumped on her bike and took off. I didn't want you to think I took up with someone else."

"Glad you told me. I imagine by the time I hit Sweaty's I'll hear you did the mattress dance with at least a good forty percent of the female population."

"Ah, small towns. I was wondering if we could rerun tonight's date?"

Ruby shook her head as Darcy debated the time. "Not tonight. We already provided the locals with enough to talk about."

"Fair enough. Tomorrow night?"

"I work at Sweaty's till eleven."

"Hmmm, all right. I guess I can settle for being your number one customer."

"Sounds good. See you then." She powered down the phone and swung around to see Ruby smirking at her.

"Not leaving town tomorrow, huh?"

"Not tomorrow, but soon. Don't put off making plans. We need to check out the surrounding cities. Right now, I need my outfit for the library. Where is it?"

"Ah, that." She grimaced. "Dumpster."

"You threw it away!"

"It needed throwing away."

"That's beside the point. I'll have to wash it if I can rescue it"

"You can't. Not after I poured maple syrup and bleach on it."

"Ruby!"

Her friend wrapped one arm around her shoulder. "I know recently I've been gone more than I've been here, but friends don't allow friends to wear ugly clothes."

"I understand, but I had a reason behind the clothes."

"Now, Darcy, if you think it was going to make everyone think you're a virgin. That dog won't hunt. Keith Dobbins told everyone he popped your cherry back in eleventh grade. It happened in his pickup truck at the drive-in movie."

"That rat bastard told everyone?"

"I never mentioned it to you since I knew you'd react this way. Tell me why you need ugly clothes."

"It's a disguise."

"Disguise, huh." Ruby gave her a squeeze. "You sound shit-faced, but you always held your liquor better than most."

Darcy sighed. This was the usual reaction she received when she tried to tell people something out of the ordinary. Not only did she have a reputation as a tall tale teller, but she also earned the label, boozehound too.

Chapter Thirteen

D ARCY ADDED ANOTHER swipe of mascara aware she might not be able to rush home before her shift at the sports bar. Her clean referee uniform complete with whistle waited on the bed. Normally, she didn't do the full makeup or smooth on leg bronzer for her job since she'd long since given up meeting anyone acceptable. Her attitude was people had to take as she was or not at all. Recently, it had been not at all, which hurt some, but didn't matter too much since she didn't plan to be in Monrovia much longer.

Ruby stood behind her making faces in the mirror. "Isn't that shirt a bit too colorful for the library?"

The fuchsia shirt decorated with several tropical blossoms did demand attention. Normally, it would have stayed in the closet. Today, she might see Killian in the library, especially since the forecast predicted rain. The man hadn't been clear on his work. She assumed it was outside.

"It's not like it will yell. Besides, I doubt there will anyone in the library to see it."

Her remark resulted in her friend hooting with laughter. "Oh, that's rich. There will be tons of people dropping by. There will be the men you refused to date coming around for a second chance."

Darcy shook her head, refusing to acknowledge the possibility.

"Deny it all you want, but you know it is true. There'll be another wave of men you did go out with it, but never got any action. Of course, they may be up for another go, too."

The idea made her moan. "Please, tell me no."

The mirror reflected by Ruby's waving hands. "I haven't even finished. Women will stop by. All the girls you went to school with will stop by probably with youngsters in tow just to check out that you're not the cold fish they always assumed you were."

"Cold fish?" It wasn't much better than tall tale spinner or booze hound. "Come on, you have to be exaggerating."

Her friend's eyebrows danced as she smirked. "Am I? Consider there isn't all that much to entertain the citizens."

"How about the minister of the Lutheran Church is a jewel thief?" If she was in danger from the known thieves, wouldn't it be better for other people to know, especially if she vanished?

"Oh, I see what you're doing. Trying to distract with rumors. No one will buy it. You'd have more luck with Tammy Lynne being pregnant by one of the bronc busters who came through town with the rodeo."

"Everyone knows that. It wouldn't exactly be gossip. It's not fair that when I tell someone the truth, no one believes me."

Ruby leaned forward, touched her ears, and moved her fingers upward indicating elongated ears. Darcy slapped her friend's hands away.

"Stop it. If you would have seen them you would have sworn they resembled elves, too."

"No, I wouldn't have." Her nose crinkled. "I wouldn't have minded seeing them since you thought they were handsome. Besides, they could have worn some costume ears. You can get those almost anywhere. Rather clever if you think that is all they did. Rather like wearing zombie contacts or vampire fangs. Enough to freak someone out."

No need to say whom Ruby meant. "So why couldn't they be elves?"

"Duh, they don't *exist.*" Ruby emphasized the last word.

"We assume they don't." Darcy ran her brush through her thick waves. "I would have told you a man who was thoughtful, handsome, and kind didn't exist, but there's Killian."

"Ah, I see your point, but how much do you really know about him. As nice as he is to look at, he could have some deep dark secret that might turn your stomach."

Surely, Ruby had to be teasing. "Like what?"

"He could hate cats."

Sylvester gave a plaintive mew, adding in his feelings on the subject.

"That would be a deal breaker. He's never said anything about cats, pro or con. Some men don't even think about pets. Too busy with their lives to give it much thought." Killian must have been the same since he was in town only for a brief project. The thought of the man had Darcy tugging her shirt downward revealing cleavage.

"I know your boss would not approve of you giving the girls a public airing. She practically throws herself against the library doors to prevent my entry in my everyday clothes."

AUNT LETICIA GRUMBLED about someone she dubbed Mark Twain wannabe as she levered a waffle out of the iron. "I'm not sure why I put up with her antics. Probably because no one else will work for so little hours or money. It could be because her mother and I have been friends forever, but her latest antics are a bit too much."

Ah, Killian knew she wanted him to comment, but he could see no use involving himself in local gossip. He poured himself a cup of coffee and inhaled the aroma. "You do have a way with coffee."

"It's the chicory. People started using it to stretch out their coffee bean supply when it became dear during the Civil War."

Ah, good ol' Aunt Leticia could turn anything into a history lesson. The woman must have been a frustrated teacher. It made him wonder why she'd never had children. Then again, the little ones would have annoyed her with their loud voices and sticky fingers.

"It's supposed to rain today. I've already decided what supplies I need so I'll buy those. Might even start on painting the back bedroom the robin egg blue you picked out."

"That would be nice." She slid a plate loaded with warm waffles onto the table. "I'd like the trim to be an off white, but there are so many versions of white now days. Could you pick up some paint chips for me to compare against the finished wall?"

"I could." He poured maple syrup over his waffle. "I'm heading into Wilsonville. Maybe I could bring you lunch."

"Lunch?" His aunt turned slowly from the counter. Her lips corners started upward, then firmed, before winging upward again. "It's been a while since anyone brought me lunch. I'd like that."

It probably been years since his aunt had smiled in delight about something. Even though she appeared to be crotchety, difficult woman, she could be kind at times. Thankfully, her waffles were better than her tuna casserole. "Appreciate you making me breakfast. Do you cook breakfast every morning?"

"Used to." Leticia poured herself a cup of coffee and joined Killian at the table. "Back when your uncle was alive. He was a big proponent of breakfast. Well, make that every meal. The man loved to eat. After his death, I stopped making breakfast. Sometimes, I even skip dinner. I make do with a bowl of cereal or a can of soup. It doesn't seem worth the trouble to cook for one person."

"Ah, I hear ya there." After Heather left, there hadn't been very many regular meals, not that she'd done any cooking while she'd been there. He didn't since he had no appetite. "I appreciate your cooking. What can I bring you from Wilsonville?"

Leticia put down her cup as she considered. "There used to be a fish place there. They had a lighthouse at the end of the building. A whitefish sandwich would be terrific."

"Sounds good. Fries? Onion rings?"

"They used to have fried okra, mushrooms, and cauliflower. They'd put the bunch altogether in a cup with a spicy dipping sauce."

It was reminiscent of bar food. "I bet my uncle loved the place."

"He did. Of course, his doctor would have warned him against it, telling him the food was too salty or heavy."

Not too surprising, most physicians would have given the fast food restaurant two thumbs down.

"Herman loved it. I figured he should eat what he wanted. If a person doesn't enjoy life, what is the use?"

The words surprised him. He would have bet his aunt was one to always follow the rules. "You have a point there. What would you do to enjoy yourself?"

"Same question I've been asking myself. I didn't expect Herman to die when he did. I'll give the man credit. He enjoyed life. In some ways, I wish I could be more like him. There are places I would like to travel to such as Ireland, but I wouldn't want to go alone."

He shoveled in more waffle as he considered his aunt's statement. "Ya know there's a good half of the family planning to hit the emerald isle. Part of them are doing some historical research, but I bet they'd love to have you come along."

"Really?" Her face brightened as she put down her coffee cup and clapped her hands together. "I'm certainly glad you decided to visit me while you were waiting to see if you still have a career."

Yeah, just like that he remembered why everyone avoided his aunt. Her habit of plain speaking tended to highlight people's fears and shortcomings. Only last night, he received a call from headquarters stating that one of the Heather's henchmen swore that Killian knew about the operation from the start. He didn't. It would be a real hoot to be inside with various offenders that he'd put behind bars. Good chance Heather told them he was a dirty cop.

"It was just luck I ended up here."

Chapter Fourteen

D ARCY CHECKED OUT the book and handed it back to a leering teenage boy. "Here you go, Trad. Didn't know today was a school holiday."

"It's not. I'm at lunch." He waggled his eyebrows. "I prefer older women."

Seriously? A few men who had her asked out in the past showed up, along with a few former classmates, now mothers, arrived pushing baby strollers. Ruby hadn't predicted this underage Romeo. "Good to know. I'll notify my grandmother."

"Wait, ah," he blustered as she turned away to duck into the office for a well-earned break from public scrutiny. Now she knew what the two-headed cow born at Jorgenson's farm must have felt like. A quick glance at the clock showed she'd endured inspections longer than the calf had. The poor creature only lived for a few hours. Geesh, what was with the male population? If the hurry up weddings were any indica-tion, she knew she wasn't the only one to get frisky in the park. It was rare to have a wedding without a pregnant bride.

A stack of books about Ireland sat at the end of the reference desk. Leticia had a large map spread out and examined it with a magnifying glass. Every now and then, she'd circle a name and created a dotted line to connect it to the previous name.

If Darcy didn't know better, she would think the woman was

planning a trip. No way would Leticia Blankenship ever leave town.

Darcy could hide out in the circulation office until someone came to the desk. The tinted glass allowed her to see the circulation desk, reference desk, and the front doors. A smiling Killian entered the front door carrying a fast food sack. The way he half-turned when he entered meant he was searching for her. Did she tell him she worked at the library? She made a step toward the open office door when jewel thief number one followed Killian in. Even if she hadn't overheard the conversation, the man would stick out like a sore thumb. If the general population resembled pet dogs, this man was a wolf, an angry one, too.

Why was he here? Darcy lingered beside the doorway, unwilling to expose herself until the man disappeared. The minister entered a few minutes later, cast furtive glances around him before moving off to the stacks. The man couldn't look guiltier if he tried. Suddenly, the library was the hub of activity, criminal and otherwise.

Surely, Killian came to see her. It looked like he brought her lunch. What a sweetheart. All she had to do was locate the man without being noticed, which might be harder than she suspected, considering the size of the library. Most of the patrons settled into the comfy couches on the left side of the circulation desk to read the newspapers and magazines. She'd exit to the right where wire racks held paperback romances and a few avid readers scanning first chapters.

As she left the paperback section, she spotted Killian leaning over the reference desk, talking to Leticia and pointing to something on the map. The fast food bag stood open as the head librarian withdrew a wrapped sandwich. He hadn't brought Darcy lunch. Her stomach made a small complaint, anticipating something a bit more exciting than her normal peanut butter and jelly sandwich.

Worse, Killian knew Leticia. How could that have happened? Right now, the woman could be relating some of her more colorful escapades. As a child, her overactive imagination amused and charmed people. Somewhere between her sixteenth and eighteenth birthday, people started to whisper about William getting the brains, while she may have taken a headfirst tumble from the changing table.

Darcy picked up some abandoned books lying on various surfaces as if that was her intention all along. She was almost to the circulation desk when jewel thief number one popped out from the non-fiction section, startling her into stillness. His eyes moved over her as he continued walking. Her minister followed and nodded at her.

"Good day, Darcy."

"And to you." His appearance along with his normal greeting prompted her usual response.

Baldy swung around and glared at her. She didn't need to see him since she could feel his stare burning holes in her back.

The jewel thieves spoke, reluctant to acknowledge one another in public.

"Who was that? Why did you talk to her?"

"She's a member of my congregation. It would be odd not to talk to her. That would attract more attention."

Darcy opened a book she held and pretended to read the first page as she eavesdropped on the conversation. Her fears about observation on a previous visit had no basis. Neither one of them had noticed her.

"I see your point. The sooner you turn over the jewels. The sooner you can go back to being shepherd of your little flock."

"Go. We can't stand here talking. I'll call you tonight with directions."

Directions. If he was giving directions, then there must be emeralds hidden somewhere in the town. If she could find them, not only would it validate her story, and she'd no longer be the crazy twin. There also might be a reward. She turned another page in her book.

"Do that. Do you think your parishioner is listening to us?

That was her clue to move. Killian headed for the exit before she could get his attention. Running after him, shouting his name wasn't an option. The last thing she wanted to do was gather anyone else's notice, especially the jewel thieves. Darcy drifted in the direction of the reference desk where Leticia munched on her sandwich.

"Special delivery lunch?"

Leticia glanced up and waved her sandwich. "Delicious sandwich from over at Wilsonville. My nephew brought it to me."

"Your nephew?" She swallowed hard, hoping she didn't sound as alarmed as she felt at the information. Killian had not mentioned his relationship to Leticia, her mercurial boss, but then again, it had never come up in conversation.

"Yes." Leticia took a bite of her sandwich, narrowed her eyes as she chewed. After, she finally swallowed, she spoke. "Don't go getting any ideas. Killian's here to recover from a bullet wound and a broken heart."

Bullet wound? "Who'd shoot at him?" Perhaps someone against construction in a wild area could be the culprit.

Leticia wrinkled her nose as if she smelled something horrible. "A criminal, of course. That's what the police do, flush out the bad guys to keep us safe."

"He's a cop?" Just this morning she told Ruby how rare it was to find a decent, honest man. Obviously, it was rarer than she thought.

"Yes." Leticia wadded up her lunch wrapper and stuffed it in the bag. "Don't tell me you're one of those women who throw themselves at police officers?"

"I'm not."

"Just as well. Killian is too smart to get involved with you. From what I hear, you have some stranger with a fast car to keep you company."

Her boss hadn't connected the dots, but neither had she. Sometimes, she considered herself smarter than the average townie. She wasn't. A pair of broad shoulders and soulful eyes caused her to abandon her usual caution. "Oh, that's just gossip. No truth to it. It's just a story I made up to keep Ronny at a distance." For once, her ability to fabricate served her.

"Good. You should avoid strangers. I'm sure your mother would tell you they never have your best interests at heart."

"You're right."

Normally, she found it hard to agree with her boss, but not today. The woman had no clue that the lying stranger was also her nephew. Her earlier enthusiasm at seeing Killian died a fast death, replaced with bitterness that settled in the back of her throat. If money wasn't an issue, she'd blow off her shift. Maybe this was what she needed, a shove to get her out of town. With any luck, Killian wouldn't show tonight.

Chapter Fifteen

ALL THE TABLES were full at Sweaty's, forcing the incoming customers to stand at the bar. The televisions blared various games, adding to the already raucous noise level. Darcy weaved her way through the men and past the brooding bald man sitting alone with his phone on the table. He could be waiting for directions. Monrovia had no motels, which forced the jewel thief to use the only real restaurant as his waiting spot. Even though, he probably wasn't staring at her, it didn't stop the hairs on her neck from standing up every time she shouldered a heavy drink tray within his visual range.

A table near the kitchen opened up. If none of the men crowded around the bar noticed it, then her load would be marginally lighter. A dark head appeared above the others as its owner weaved his way toward her. No. Not now. He was the last person she wanted to see. A familiar voice called out.

"There's my sister."

William popped out the crowd and waved at her.

Her brother, not Killian. What a relief. She angled her head at the empty table. William slid into the chair with a grin and motioned to someone in the crowd. Elaine, she assumed, but it would be rather rude to force her to fend for herself among a group of sports crazy half-drunk fans.

The sexy Black Irish cop parted the crowd with ease and sat down with her brother. William gestured to Killian. "I met your friend at a hardware shop in Wilsonville. He was getting supplies to some construction work on his aunt's house."

She slapped down the plastic laminated menus on the table and glared at Killian. "Construction, huh?"

"Darcy. Behave. I know our mother taught you better."

She had, and they were in public. Any one of the patrons would be happy to report to her mother that she was being a little less than civil. "True." She gave her brother a confirming nod before she turned her attention to Killian. "She also told me to ignore liars." She asked her brother while keeping her back to Killian, "What can I get you?"

"The Sweets Platter."

Her pen hovered over her pad, but she couldn't resist teasing her brother, especially since he brought in the one person she didn't want to see. "What was that?"

"The Sweet Cheeks platter with fries. Cola."

Darcy's intention to leave without taking Killian's order was foiled by the jewel thief pushing past her. She leaned in over the table trying to make herself as small as possible. Killian's mouth was inches from her ear as he leaned in to speak to her.

"I didn't lie to you. I told you I was doing construction. I am. On my aunt's house."

When he said it, the explanation somehow made sense. "You never mentioned being a cop or that you'd been shot and had your heart broken."

William echoed her. "You were shot?"

Jewel thief behind her murmured, "Cop."

Yeah, if anyone should be alarmed about a cop, it should be him, not her. Maybe she should tell Killian about the thieves.

Killian groaned, even though she knew it wasn't meant to be erotic. Her body still reacted to his guttural utterance.

"It had to be my aunt. What did she say?"

"Pretty much what I already said."

His splayed hand covered his face. "Sweet Jesus. I thought my mother tended to meddle. It never occurred to me that it ran in the family."

William laughed. "While I do admit to enjoying the show, I hope you might put my order in. Maybe even take Killian's. I told Elaine I'd be by later tonight to approve the wedding colors."

The fact her brother even thought he had input about the colors amused her. "Good luck with that. Don't tell her you had your heart set on teal and silver when she picked raspberry and apricot."

She sashayed to the kitchen certain Killian watched her. He should be a rat bastard in her eyes, but he made everything sound so reasonable. At no time had she asked if he was a policeman. There was a big difference between a cop and deputy. At least, she hoped there was.

Clyde had a tiny television mounted right above the grill. The cook held up his spatula aloft caught up in a news report in the middle of flipping a burger.

"What has caught your interest?"

"Jailbreak."

"Not near here?" The closest jail was twenty miles away. Whenever some good ol' boys got too rowdy, they were released to their wives or mother depending on their age.

"Nope. Not too close. Newscaster talked about them being bad news. Cop killers. No reason for them to head to our little village."

The thought made her shudder. Clyde had a valid assumption, but he was unaware jewel thieves were already among them. A cop killer would be ruthless. Perhaps, she should warn Killian. After handing over her order and picking up two finished platters, she threaded her way to the bar to pick up the beers.

On her way back, she'd tell Killian, but she didn't expect him to do anything, especially if he was on vacation. Working her way back, however, was more of a thought than a possibility. The crowd was so thick she had to elbow her way through the excited fans. Apparently, an underdog team grabbed the ball and ran with it. Not too surprising that everyone became underdog fans.

Since all eyes were on the television, she couldn't get anyone to move to let her through. Finally, in desperation Darcy exited through the front the door. The noise abated a little on the outside.

The cooler air energized her as she speculated about not returning. If she and Ruby were heading out of town, what difference would a few days make. Still, as one of two working waitresses, the tips would be good. Besides, she needed to warn Killian.

Another car parked down the street. She could have discouraged the people from coming due to the lack of seating, but there really wasn't any place else to go. Whoever it was, wasn't walking her way. Instead, the silhouettes of people surrounded a car before moving on to the next vehicle. It could be someone checking to see if her husband was where he said he would be. It was hard to tell if the people were women, but at least one was. Tired of trying to analyze the lurkers' actions, she rounded the building to slip in the backdoor the same time the jewel thief slipped out.

Darcy flattened herself against the building, hiding in the shadows. The man jogged past not bothering to look her way. Maybe the minister finally gave up the information regarding the jewels' location. Then again, the placid smiling man who shook her hand every Sunday could be much more complex than she ever imagined. Even now he could be boarding a plane to somewhere tropical while texting the coordinates to the middle of a cornfield.

The platters were up when Darcy ducked into the kitchen. Clyde pivoted at the slam of the door.

"Did you get lost?"

"Nope. It was easier to go all the way around as opposed to fighting my way through a wall of sports fan. I see my order is up."

"You bet. I noticed your brother's fiancé is here. She'll probably want something to eat too."

Normally, she might agree, but a female determined to be married would be on a diet, which would mean she would try to lose weight to fit into a much smaller size than she would normally. She'd get by on a few of William's fries, a bite of his burger, or a sip of his beer. In the end, her brother would order another platter.

"Do me a favor, Clyde and load the Sweet Cheeks platter up with some more fries. You know Elaine is going to snarf them down why insisting she wants nothing."

The cook did as she asked, then snorted. "For a woman, you tell it like it is."

"That's right. I do. Why does no one ever believe me?"

Clyde's fingers went to his ears.

"Oh, please, not the elf thing again. How many times have I told everyone something real that did happen and they forget? What about the flash flood, the runaway combine, or the rabid raccoon?"

"All true." Clyde agreed. He held up one finger. "You know people fixate on what's more interesting or exotic. That's why they forget the ordinary."

"Hmm, just an excuse to exaggerate stories, especially when they involve me."

"Hah, it is more like when they involve anyone. Remember that."

Chapter Sixteen

CIGARETTE SMOKE WAFTED through the air, causing Killian to twist in the hard-plastic seat to see who the offender was. There was a sea of male shoulders encased in plaid shirts, T-shirts, and the occasional denim jacket. Whoever was smoking felt free to do so since no one could get to him in this crowd. The town of Monrovia could easily support another sports bar. He didn't understand how Darcy could manage working in such a place. Still, being a small town, employment options were few. Those who didn't farm, drove to manufacturing jobs in nearby bigger towns.

So far, the only women he spotted in town we're pushing baby strollers or walking children to the bus stops. That's if you discounted the waitresses here, Ruby, his Aunt Leticia, and the determined female on the bike. In some ways, the town could either be lost in time or an episode of a sci-fi drama where the women were all hidden away. Speaking of women, he nodded at Elaine, who'd joined them because she couldn't stand to be away from her sweetie pie, William.

"So, after the wedding, what are your career plans?"

The woman stared at him as if he spoke another language, blinked twice, then managed an indulgent smile. The kind one gives an ignorant child or the very stupid. "I'll be a supportive wife." She gave William's arm a squeeze before tacking on, "Mother, too."

He wondered for a second if William was on board with the mother thing, but the gentle pat he delivered to his clutching fiancée's hand assured he was. Not sure of the proper response, he murmured, "Well, that's nice." It sounded lame to his own ears.

Elaine Rickbed her head in agreement. "When the kids start school, I'll have my own dance and tumbling studio. I was part of the high school dance team. All little girls should have the privilege of shaking their pom-poms."

The laugh that bubbled up behind his teeth, he managed to swallow, realizing Elaine was serious about shaking the pom-poms and didn't realize it could be interpreted another way. Besides, wasn't it weird enough he was already sitting here with the brother of the woman he played imaginary strip poker with less than twenty-four hours ago?

William approached him in the hardware store introducing himself as Darcy's brother. Even if he hadn't seen him in the bar, the family resemblance was there. Instead of punching him in the nose, between screws and wall anchors, William conversed in a moderate tone of voice about his sister. He discussed Darcy's dreams of being a writer, her issues with fitting in, and what she wanted. If Killian was what she wanted right now, then William was on-board, so much so her brother gave him the keys to their family lakeside cabin. William explained, while he pretended to look at rope, that it would keep Darcy out of the public eye. He probably assumed due to his besotted state that everyone else should be likewise.

His fingers traced over the outline of the key in his front jeans pocket. After last night, he doubted he would even need the key, but William urged him to hold onto it. He could always leave it for Darcy, who would place it back under the flowerpot on the cabin porch.

Just about the time he mused about Darcy's location for about the sixth time, she strolled toward him carrying a heavy round tray over her head. Some of the men made a scooting side step to let her by, a few others didn't. One wiggled his fingers as preparing to touch her as she went by. Killian forced a cough, caught the handsy man's eye, who wisely chose to insert his hand into his pocket.

"Here you go." She placed the platters in front of them. William got the one with a mountain of fries. Darcy rounded her mouth when she saw Elaine practically sitting on her brother's lap. "Oh, Elaine, I didn't know you were here."

What an awful liar, then again as a cop, the people he met sometimes depended on their lies keeping them out of jail and other times keeping them alive. They were motivated liars.

Elaine giggled. "You know I couldn't stand being away from your brother." She turned adoring eyes on her sweetheart. "I don't need anything. Got to watch my weight for the wedding." She picked up a fry and waved it as she spoke.

Even though her actions made Killian want to make gagging noises, he realized his reaction might be due to no one ever feeling that way about him as opposed to the ridiculousness of Elaine's behavior. Darcy turned amused eyes to him. So, he wasn't the only one.

"Can I get you anything, Killian?"

Her lips practically massaged his name. He found himself transfixed by her perfect mouth coated in a shiny lip gloss. "Ah, yes. You could say my name again."

Another foot, not his own, connected with his ankle. William, probably reminding him of the key in his pocket. Elaine giggled. Again. "How sweet. Do you think she'll really say it?"

Darcy stood clutching the empty tray against her side. Just about the time he expected her to pivot and walk away, she bent and put her mouth close to his ear.

Her breathy voice whispered, "Killian."

When he thought, it couldn't get any better, she added on. "You lie."

Ah, not that. His hand snagged hers before she could whirl away. William wrapped his arms around Elaine and nuzzled her, giving him a tiny bit of privacy in the crowded bar. "Let me explain. I had my reasons. If you knew, you'd understand."

"Ah, yeah, I bet. You wouldn't be doing any explaining with your hands or with that very nice body of yours, would you?"

It was hard to know how to answer. He thought he knew the right answer, but her eyes twinkled. Was she teasing him? "It would all depend on what you wanted. Tonight, you call the shots."

The wrist he held turned in his grip, allowing her fingers to stroke his wrist as she spoke. "I'd like that. Calling the shots, I mean."

He grinned when her lips tipped up. Success. He didn't expect to get another chance, even though Darcy's brother urged him on. Twins were supposed to have a special communication. Did William inherently know how Darcy felt? Could the brother detect something he couldn't see? He glanced at William, who had the bottom half of his face encased in Elaine's hair. The man winked at him.

Maybe he winked at Darcy. Then again, it could be a trick of the lighting. Did she even know he had the key to the family cabin? There were so many things he wanted to ask her, but not here, especially in front of her brother.

A cool sensation climbed up his spine putting him on alert. His eyes darted around the room. Men stood shoulder to shoulder, hefting beers as they stared in the direction of the half dozen televisions mounted on the walls. Nothing had changed. Well, at least nothing he could see. All his life, he knew when things were going to happen. It was a feeling, a premonition.

Darcy loosened his hold on her wrist and drifted away into the sea of testosterone where he knew other men fantasized about her as she pushed past them. His muscles tightened as he surveyed the crowd looking for one leering man. Not surprisingly, any man that met his eye looked away immediately. The tingling came again. Weird. He had nothing to be afraid of, especially here. Maybe his cop sense wasn't as good as it used to be. Come on, he let Heather put one over on him. He grimaced at the thought. Besides, being hot, Heather really wasn't much else. Neither his mother or partner had been a fan. Could be they saw her for what she was since they weren't using his glasses fogged by equal amounts of lust and longing. The lust was understand-able, but the longing even bewildered him a little.

He knew he could meet a woman, chat her up, and spend the night with her. That wasn't the nature of his longing. The whispered voices of William and Elaine reminded him. He wanted someone who he had inside jokes with, ate his fries while denying doing it, and couldn't stand not being by his side. As a cop, there were groupies. Women got off on the uniform, the badge, and the gun. No, he didn't want that at all. Yeah, he chose not to talk about being a cop, not the same as lying. He just wanted to be liked for who he was, not what he was.

As for his premonition, maybe it had been working when he was with Heather, but he chose to ignore it. He made excuses for her when she vanished without a note. Even when her disappearing act coincided with neighborhood burglaries he refused to believe and talked himself out of his suspicions. Heather intentionally inserted herself in his life, knowing his current beat was narcotics.

Okay. Flight or fight response I hear you now. Sorry. I ignored you before. Could you calm it down, please? Maybe he needed another beer. Instead of having Darcy fetch it, he could get it himself.

"WE'RE OUT OF hard cider." Rick yelled across the room in Darcy's direction. "Could you check in the back room to see if we have any more?"

She nodded, made a turn to the back room, while grumbling to herself. Her feet hurt. The crowd never abated. For every two people who left, three more men shouldered their way inside. Rick didn't need to add if she found cider that she needed to haul it to the bar. It was a given. What they needed was more help.

Only those hard up for a job worked at Sweaty's. The only males included the bartenders and the cook. As for the women, most didn't want the rep that went along with being a cocktail waitress. Somehow, church people had equated serving beer and wearing a garish outfit with being a hooker. No one wanted that attached to their name, especially if they expected to marry someday. Desperate souls like herself who needed the money took the job. Sometimes, the tips could be very good. Still, they never balanced out a hellacious night like tonight. She flicked on the light in the storeroom and meandered through the cylinders reading brand names.

The closed-circuit television monitors displayed the front room from various angles. She never saw the reason for installing the monitors in the supply room, but originally, it was going to be the manager's office. She located the needed cider and wrestled it on a dolly for moving it.

Maybe she could see Killian on the monitor. There were three cameras. One pointed at the front entrance, another at the back, and the third at the bar. There had been a fourth in the kitchen, but Clyde *accidentally* broke it as soon as it went up.

The black and white images didn't offer revelations or any close-ups of a certain handsome cop. The word still made her grit her teeth, but he promised to explain. The minister and his wife sitting at a back table surprised her, especially when she saw his partner in crime leave. Something was happening. Being out in public where he could be seen could serve as an alibi.

The front door swung open, and two more people entered, stood, and surveyed the room. Definitely not locals since she would have known them. The hard-faced blonde didn't fit in here, neither did her hipster friend with the carefully groomed beard. If a Monrovia male sported a beard, and they often did during harvest season, it was because they didn't waste time shaving.

Peculiar. She stared at the two, wondering what they were about until the buzzer startled her. The electronic buzzer served as little more than a doorbell. It could be pushed at the bar to signal a need for help or cider, as in her case. By the time, she wheeled it up there, Rick would need something else.

At five foot five, Darcy never saw above the patron's heads until she reached the raised bar. The extra six inches allowed her the ability to make out the door. The strangers were gone. It was hard to tell if they'd blended into the crowd. Still, a non-local woman would have caused a stir, especially a looker. It didn't matter if she showed up with a guy. The patrons would still manage furtive glances on their way to the restroom or the jukebox.

Rick heaved a sigh of relief as she pushed the cylinder in front of her. "Thank you. It must be the season change, but everyone and their brother wants cider."

Otis, the other bartender, added, "That is when they don't want whiskey. Could you check and see if there is any fireball whiskey left?"

Are you kidding me? She didn't say the words, but Otis took a step back as if her mind shouted it. He waved the request away. "Never mind, if they can't drink straight whiskey, they don't need any."

Yeah, she would have said the same, but only because she didn't fancy another trip to the supply room. The shrill bell cut through the noise, signaling an order up. Great. All she had to do was make it through the night. Darcy slid into the kitchen for breathing room and picked up her order from the wrong side of the window. At least, it gave her some space.

"Tired of being a celebrity?" Clyde asked as he smoked his forbidden cigar. Normally, he would have waited for a smoke break, but no time tonight.

"Me?" She pointed to herself before reaching for the grilled cheese and onion rings platter. She centered it on the tray before adding the chicken wings.

"Yeah, you. Everyone knows Ronny comes every night to announce his claim to you. After last night, people thought there might be a fight. At the very least, they bet money on if the new guy would be here to stare everyone down, taking over where Ronny left off."

"People bet on it?" Her already hot face flushed more if that were even possible. Her blood pressure spiked. "Clyde, you didn't?" She threw the cook a questioning glance.

"Hey," he complained around his cigar. "I lost money. I bet on Ronny. How did I know your brother would show up with the new guy? He approved him. A stranger, too."

"That's what that's all about? What would have happened if William hadn't showed up with Killian?"

"Ha. Almost anything. Depends on the mood of the crowd and the amount of beer drunk. Nothing could have happened. Ronny could have riled the crowd up against the man who is staring down anyone who dares look at you for more than five seconds."

"Killian does that?" There did seem to be quite a few less hands feeling her anatomy tonight. Ronny, generally liked by everyone, did not have a reputation as a fighter. Killian, a stranger, was an unknown.

"You think my brother came in with Killian by accident?"

"Nope." Clyde stubbed out his cigar and reached for the spatula. "The grilled cheese is getting cold, and it never reheats well."

Darcy delivered the food, thinking even the town she thought she knew so well had layers. One of those layers had people betting on her sex life. She could have done without that one. So far, everyone would be sadly disappointed, including her.

Chapter Seventeen

B Y TEN-THIRTY, RICK rang the last call chime. Other places might have waited until ten till eleven before doing so, but Sweaty's patrons could nurse a beer for a good thirty minutes. Some didn't want to leave the camaraderie of their fellows. Others hoped to avoid some recriminations from their spouse. Still others, usually the bachelor farmers, had nothing to go home to, which was the main reason they were there in the first place. Elaine had towed her brother from the bar an hour earlier.

Killian waited for her, sitting with his hands around an empty beer mug, hiding the state of it. He refused a refill the last three times she asked. The knowledge he wanted to be fully functional made parts of her join a conga line, but a mirrored liquor sign stopped the dance party. Even in a dimly lit mirror, her bedraggled hair and tired expression wouldn't win her any beauty contests. There had to be something she could do to improve matters.

Since she usually changed into her waitress outfit at work, at least she could change out of her beer soaked shirt. Twenty minutes later, she scrubbed her face with a cheap paper towel wiping away the mascara smut. A few patrons slumped against the bar. Their slurred voices indicating a need for a ride home. Monrovia didn't have a cab service. If married, Otis would call their wives. Occasionally, a girlfriend might be called to ferry her drunken suitor home. Girlfriends could be problematic since the female might not consider the relationship serious enough to provide pickup services. Other times, Otis and Rick drove the sloshed men home.

She exited the bathroom to discover Killian helping the men collect bottles and glasses. Sweaty didn't pay overly well and made the women dress in questionable outfits, but he did let them leave at closing time. The way he saw it, no customers, no need for women servers. Sometime in the wee hours, a cleaning company arrived and wiped the place clean. The antiseptic smell would greet them the next day.

Darcy had never met the cleaners. She thought of them as fairies or brownies who appeared when everyone was asleep, cleansed the place of sweat and spilled alcohol stink.

Killian joked with the bartenders and remaining customers as he wiped down a table. "My uncle owned a bar." He offered as an explanation. "I often helped him clean up at closing time."

Otis showed some interest, probably due to his often-voiced comment of opening his own bar someday. "Oh, really. What was it called?"

"The Blue Line."

Otis and Rick exchanged confused looks, but no one had to explain to Darcy that it was a cop bar. Law enforcement must run in his family. Well, that made a difference. The man wasn't a bully who needed a gun and a badge to throw his weight around. She watched him as she shouldered a heavy tray of empties and carried them to the bar.

The other waitress skirted her tables, pocketing her tips. She passed Darcy on her way out. "He's a good one."

"Yeah, I'm starting to figure that out." Maybe she never settled on anyone because she always had all these reasons a man wouldn't work out. Then again, it could have been she'd hadn't bumped up against the right one. Sweaty's was the last place open on a weeknight. She didn't fancy another night in the park or driving to the next city for a fast food burger.

When her brother left, he gave her shoulder a playful punch and mentioned looking out for her, whatever that meant. Had he had a heart to heart talk with Killian? If so, the man didn't spook easy.

Otis was the first to notice her. He nudged Killian, who glanced her way. "Time to go. See you guys later."

The men chuckled as if they shared some great joke. They assumed he'd get lucky. With any luck, they both would, if they could only pin down a location. The man must own a house or an apartment, but she had no clue how far away it was. Killian reached her, pushed something in her hand, and raised one inquiring eyebrow.

The gold toned house key with a fleck of purple nail polish on it belonged to the family's lakeside cabin. The cabin, how could she have forgotten? Even though they spent many summer weekends in it, her visits fell off as she reached adulthood. Outside of a bachelorette party, she threw for a friend a couple of years back, she hadn't been inside. The place could be a mouse hotel for all she knew. Her fingers wrapped around the key. "William?"

Killian nodded.

Then it would be okay. She wouldn't be surprised if Elaine and William left early to fix the place up. The newly engaged couple probably used the cabin a great deal for privacy since Elaine lived at home and William had a roommate.

"What are we waiting for?" Except maybe food. Her stomach growled, reminding she hadn't a chance for supper on her six-hour shift.

Clyde held out a white fast food bag, which she took. Technically, as part of her job she was allowed a burger. The only difference was she was taking it with her. The weight of the bag announced it was more like a feast for three or four people. "Thanks."

They exited out the back door, avoiding the cameras. No reason to get anyone in trouble. "Did William tell you where the cabin is?"

"He told me you would know."

"Let's say it's a rough road. Could be muddy in places since rain is expected. Why don't we take my car? I know the way."

"Would you still respect my masculinity if you drive?"

They stepped out into the still night where her car sat in the alley near the back door. "Ah, here it is." She gestured to her aging compact that he'd already met. "It may not look like much, but it will make the trip."

At least, she hoped it would. When she bought the car used it hadn't been in that great of condition, but since her goal had always been to move to a city with public transport, the concept of sinking money she didn't have in a car did not appeal.

Killian closed the driver door for her before sliding into the passenger side. Still the gentleman, even if they were driving up to the lake to get better acquainted. There was nothing to do in Monrovia. A shower, a massage, and a drink would work wonders. Outside of a fancy spa, she didn't know where she might find two of the three.

What did a woman say to a hot man when she planned on jumping his bones or let him jump hers? The way her legs felt maybe Killian could do all the heavy lifting. She should do something seductive to set the mood. "So why did you lie to me?"

Wait a minute, that was a mood killer question, not a mood setter.

"Surprised you waited that long. Truth is I wanted not to be a cop for a while. My career may be over. I'm here in Monrovia helping my aunt with her decaying house while I wait to hear from the inquiry board."

"What happened?" Another question that would rack up negative feelings.

"The better question would be what didn't happen. It was my

worst nightmare, a real clusterfuck. It started with a woman."

Darcy exhaled, aware she wasn't going to like any story that started with a woman and Killian. "A sexy woman, I bet."

"I thought so at the time, not realizing she was more predatory than a black widow spider."

"Aren't they the spiders who eat their mates?"

"I think all female spiders eat their mates or at least try. Gotta feel for the male who is forced through desire and evolutionary forces to mate only to become a crunchy after sex snack."

The conversation needed help. Darcy slipped a hand to Killian's jean clad thigh. "You have no worries about me eating you."

"Well, that's depressing. I was rather hoping you would." He laughed. Darcy joined in, although her laughter tended to be the nervous sort, though he did dispel some of the tension. "Should I ask about the spider woman?"

"You should." He cleared his throat. "It's hard for me to talk about Heather in a normal fashion."

Heather. What a fake name. She already hated her without knowing anything about her. "Normal fashion?"

"Yeah. When I'm not being cross-examined as if somehow I was part of the whole criminal gang?"

Killian, a criminal? No way. The resentment seeped through his words. Whoever this Heather was she had a lot to answer for, including ruining her night so far. "I hate to ask. I can already hear how upset you are." His thigh muscles flexed under her hand.

He inhaled deeply, slowly blew out the breath, before speaking. "Damn it, Darcy. I like you!"

"You don't have to sound so angry about it." She pulled her hand from his thigh and wondered if she should turn the car around.

"See. It's not you. It's Heather. My stupidity." He grabbed her free hand, put it back on his thigh, and covered it with his own. "Leave your hand where it is until I finish the story. Of course, if you need it to turn left I understand."

"Go on." Her doubts about not knowing what to say faded away since Killian had a great deal to contribute.

"Anyhow, I met Heather by accident, I thought. I didn't realize until later she needed a narcotics cop. That way she could feed information to her drug buddies."

"You weren't coming home and telling her who you busted that day." She knew most women wouldn't ask.

"No. It started out with her wanting to move in with me, which was supposed to be a short time thing until she got an apartment. It wasn't a 'we're so serious about each other we need to live together'. Heather had some confused story about her roommate moving out and how she couldn't afford the apartment on her own. Once she moved in, she quit looking for affordable apartments. At the time, I thought she was cheap since she wasn't paying rent."

Other than a mooching girlfriend, she didn't understand where a bullet wound came in. Betty McGiver accidentally shot her husband in the leg when he'd been out too late one night. Everyone agreed it was accidental since the woman had won the turkey shoot three years in a row. If he'd been up to no good, she would have aimed higher. "Yeah, the bitch took advantage of you."

"You have no clue. My neighborhood is a quiet, working class neighborhood. Whenever someone went on vacation they told me, certain a cop on the lookout would keep their house safer. I even marked down who was on vacation on my kitchen calendar."

Darcy turned up Forest Road and bumped over the potholes that pitted the neglected road. "I have a bad feeling about this."

"I only wish I had at the time. I even told her to keep an eye on the houses. She served as a lookout as her drug buddies stole anything they could fence from family heirlooms to guns. The families would come back to their back doors jimmied open and their valuables missing. More than a few gave me the fisheye when it kept happening. I even called in favors, asking patrol cars to drive by. Heather cleverly urged me to do this so she'd know exactly when the car would be in the vicinity."

"Wow! What a piece of work." She flipped on her brights, catching a possum crossing the road. "Did she shoot you when you found out?" She could feel his gaze on her. "Your aunt mentioned you'd been shot."

"Yeah, right. No, that happened in a sting operation gone bad. We had some undercover guys inside and had been planning this for months Usually, I leave my work at work. My mistake was taking some calls at home. Even had my computer password protected, but I wasn't nearly as discreet as I thought. She heard enough to warn her buddies who were running a startup meth distribution web, which they funded with burglaries. Instead, of slipping away quietly into the night they decided on a showdown. Heather allowed me and my partner to walk into their trap. People used to tease my partner and me about how much we looked alike. They used to call us twins, although Jake was Hispanic while I'm Black Irish. She even kissed me when I left the house. Later, after the fire fight, I saw her fleeing the scene as I tried to stop Jake from bleeding out. I knew then I'd been played."

"How awful! Jake?" She could guess the ending.

"He died. It's my fault. If I hadn't gotten involved, Jake would still be alive today."

The man had a point. She could see why he would believe what he did, but it pained her to hear the grief in his voice. "Think for a moment. Heather would have found a way into narcotics. You weren't the only guy on the force. Plenty of men, both married and single would be flattered by her attention. You said she was hot looking?" Those weren't his exact words, but she knew men didn't normally jump through hoops for a plain woman.

"Yeah, she was, in a hard way, rather like the strippers at the gentlemen's clubs. Everything is in the right place, but their souls left a long time ago. Blonde hair, long, long legs, and a mouth… well, never mind."

Darcy could fill in the never mind part. The woman sounded like everything she wasn't. Not a blonde, not tall, but she did have a mouth. The black and white image from the monitor came to mind. "Yeah, I know the type. Tell me the rest. I can tell you're hesitating."

"Hell, yes. Before I started blabbing about Heather, I expected, we could have a fire, some wine, and whatever else might come our way." He sighed before continuing, "Now, you probably wrote me off as a fool."

She squeezed his leg. "Please, have you looked in the mirror?" She smirked before continuing. "Besides William gave you the cabin key. He has never given anyone the cabin key before you. That says a great deal. My brother is an analytical thinker. If you're stupid, a bad bet, or any combination of the two, no key. Finish the story, release the poison, and we can move on to whatever comes our way."

He leaned across the console and landed a brief kiss on her cheek. "I don't deserve you, but I have no intention of letting you go, either."

The statement pleased her immensely, making her feel like a fireball from one of those video games exploded in her chest, spreading out light to the rest of her body. "I just might hold onto you, too. The story."

"Whenever an officer discharges his gun, there is an inquiry. This is doubly true when an officer dies. The fact that I could name Heather so easily and a few of her friends that had come around made me look suspicious. They lawyered up with some slime ball attorney that probably advised them to point the finger at me, which they did."

"That's awful."

"It was. I was cleared of criminal intent, but everyone still gave me the fisheye. My close buddies still trusted me, but not everyone on the force does. Forget my neighborhood. I can't face any of them. They witnessed my house being searched and various items, including my computer and calendar seized. My mother thought the time away would help me think out what I want to do next."

Here she thought she had it bad as a teller of questionable stories. At least no one blamed her for the missing family silver or the death of their son. She didn't even want to know if Jake was married. "Have you figured out what you're going to do, yet?"

"No, I've spent my free time thinking about you." He withdrew his hand and patted his shirt pocket, then his pants. "I even forgot my phone. Darcy, when I'm around you I can't even think straight."

The car headlights caught the shimmer of the lake under a half moon. A wide turn brought the cabin into view. A light illuminated the interior while smoke puffed gently from the chimney. There'd probably be a chilled bottle of wine waiting, too. Sometimes, it was good to be a twin. Right now, it was even better to have a twin brother with a thoughtful girlfriend.

Chapter Eighteen

EATHER, HER DASTARDLY deeds, and drug buddies stories stayed outside as Killian and Darcy climbed the three steps to the porch. She had the food bag in one hand as Killian used the key to open the door. The lack of cars meant her brother and Elaine had worked their magic and left. Surprising, since they left a fire burning. Her brother probably had lookouts to warn him that the two of them were on their way.

Great that would mean everyone would know she and Killian spent the night together. She shouldn't be too upset unless they bet on that, too. The door swung open to a small table lamp burning, a hint of pine in the air, two wine glasses on the raw pine coffee table along with an opened bottle of wine.

"Looks like my fairy godparents of romance have worked their magic." She gestured to the scene.

"It all looks good." Killian closed the door and shot the bolt. "What's this?" He held up a heart shaped note that had been taped to the back of the door.

"Instructions?" It had to be from Elaine since heart notes were not her brother's style. She plucked the note out of his hand. "There's a surprise on the back deck."

"A surprise? Surprises have never been good in my experience. I guess we should look."

Something her brother had mentioned in passing had her sprinting to the deck door. "I think I know what it is." A fat candle glowed on an iron wrought table beside two fluffy towels. Darcy waited until Killian caught up with her before she opened the glass door to the deck revealing the gurgling hot tub.

She grinned at her companion. "See, all surprises aren't bad. Let's try it out." She danced out onto the deck. "A couple of weeks ago, William asked me what I thought about a hot tub at the cabin. I told him I'd probably live there if he installed one. Of course, I was joking about living here since there aren't any decent roads. I'd be trapped in the winter." She slid one hand into the heated water. "It's perfect."

She toed off her shoes, shimmied out of her jeans, and had her top off before she noticed Killian wasn't moving. "What?"

"Are you going to strip right out here on the back porch?"

"Um, yes. It's not like we have close neighbors." She reached back to unclasp her bra. "Besides, it wasn't like we were planning to keep our clothes on all night." She tossed it at Killian before kicking off her panties and jumping into the water.

"Hurry, it's heaven." She sunk down to her shoulders, but twisted around to watch Killian undress. He kept his eyes on her and unbuttoned his shirt slowly.

"Come on. The water will be cold before you're done."

His husky laugh washed over her, stimulating her already heightened senses. Both his hands gripped his opened shirt, and he spun around instead of pulling it off. The material pooled against his back as he worked his arms out, then dropped to the floor.

"Quit teasing me and get in here."

He placed one foot on the iron wrought chair and worked his boot off, then did the same with the other and peeled both socks off. "You should talk. I spent the entire night watching your cute ass wiggle through the beer soaked crowd. There was more than one randy citizen

I had to stare down."

"Oh, really?" She balanced her chin on her folded arms resting on the edge of the spa. "I didn't see you getting up and chasing them away."

"Didn't need too. A look worked." He unbuckled his belt and pulled it free of belt loops. "Besides, I had a boner I didn't want to display. Might make some of the men jealous."

"Ha. Ha." She splashed water toward him, but it fell short. "So, you used to dance. Is this a sample?"

"Not really." His fingers popped the top button on his jeans and slid the zipper down. "I'd have on clothes you could tear away. Then I'd encourage you to put your hands on me."

His leg came out in a liquid sliding step as Darcy stood up in the water. Put her hands on him? She could make that happen.

He gave a bump and grind as she slipped onto the deck.

"I'd do this." He pushed out his hips, then circled them in a lazy eight.

Before he could do anything else, Darcy embraced him from behind, splaying her wet hands on his bare chest. "Got you." Her hands slid down to his open jeans and cupped his desire. "I'm betting you'd have a G-string on for all the bills."

"Ahh, I would." The words came out on a husky breath. He pushed his jeans down as he kicked them away. "Stripper pants are easier."

"Yeah, I just bet they are." She murmured the words against his skin, then sank her teeth into his shoulder.

"You want to play rough?" He twirled, cupped his arms under her legs and back, and swung her up against his chest.

Darcy slapped his chest. "I want to play, but first you have to put me down and strip all the way. It's only fair since I'm naked. It didn't take me all night to get that way either."

"Bossy, aren't we?" He bent his knees, letting her feet touch the ground. His hands slid up from her waist, under her breasts, until his fingers tweaked one nipple. "Cold?" His warm lips replaced his fingers before she could reply.

If she had been cold, she wasn't any longer. His free hand found its way between her legs. His fingers found her clitoris and jump started her juices.

"Hmm, yes." Although, she'd already forgotten the question. Her thumbs slid inside his boxers and slowly pulled them down over his hips, but she could move them no farther, unless she wanted Killian to stop.

"A determined woman. Let me kick them off before I end up tripping before I bring you to a screaming climax. I'll end up knocking myself out, and you'll be forced to finish the job."

Darcy stepped back, but moved her hand to her breast to pull her nipple. "Better hurry. I might have to finish without you." She took another step backwards closer to the hot tub as her eyes stayed on Killian, who'd shuck his shorts. The clouds scuttled out of the way to allow the moon a chance to highlight Killian's physique.

"Very nice. Nice marble rod. I even might let you put it in me." She turned and splashed into the tub. A large splash and surge of water had her pivoting to face Killian.

They embraced, wrapping their arms tightly around each other before sinking to sit. Both heads went under the water. Darcy was propelled upward thanks to Killian lifting her. His head came up beside hers. "Seats?"

"They're in the corners. Let me show you. One is a lounger you can put stretch out on." She pulled him near the side. "The other is a seat where you can sit upright, and I can…" She waited until he lowered himself to the seat and the water lapped him mid-chest.

"You were saying." His hands fitted on her waist and pulled her onto his lap.

Darcy stretched her neck back to look full into his face. The ends of her hair floated on the water. The flickering candle cast his features into the shadow, but she'd already memorized what he looked like. The slight scent of citronella perfumed the air.

"Ah, well, I was thinking…" Her early boldness trickled away as she tried to explain one of the possibilities the seat might hold.

His hands maneuvered her until they were face to face. "Straddle me." She did, feeling his erection. She rocked forward enough to guide his length into her, then sat, filling her.

Silence reigned until the water splashed over the sides as Killian gently rocked upward. Darcy gripped his shoulders and eased herself up, then down. Tension built, as her nails sunk into his skin. Part of her, marveled that she, Darcy Darlington, was doing the wild thing in a hot tub. Together, they found a mutual rhythm. The water continued to gurgle and splash as they frolicked.

Killian bent his head and latched onto her breast as it bounced upward. His teeth abraded the nipple, heightening her desire.

"Again."

A slight turn of his head gave him access to the other breast as she lunged upward. Their play continued until they both came within seconds of one another, collapsing against each other, gasping for air.

The chill of the night wind pebbled her flesh. All she could hear was the rasp of Killian's breathing and a slight lap of the water. The jets had switched off. The water level had dropped considerably, making Darcy wonder if the jets had stopped due to the timer or the low water. She snuggled up against Killian absorbing his body warmth. "I think it is time to go inside and take advantage of the fire and the food."

She stood and swung one leg over the side of the spa the same time Killian wrapped an arm around her waist.

"Are you going to use me, then abandon me, all for warmth and a burger?"

She turned in his half-embrace and landed a kiss on his nose. "It's not just a burger. There's wine too. As for using you, there's an entire night left. Hope you're up to it."

"Always." He gave her a playful swat on the ass before releasing her.

Chapter Nineteen

KILLIAN OPENED HIS eyes, trying to remember why there was an open beam ceiling above his head. The predawn light revealed a dresser with a horse collar mirror suspended above it. The end posts of a brass bed, he could distinguish. There was a patchwork covering him and the woman snuggled up to him.

Darcy. What a mass of contradictions the woman was. Sometimes she could be bold, other times naïve, fierce, then shy. He rolled over to find her awake. Darcy spoke first.

"What are you thinking about?"

"You. Somehow everything you do is a contradiction."

"Hmm. Not sure if that is good or bad." She ran her fingers down his arm and across his chest, brushing his nipple in the process. He suspected she did it deliberately, revving him up on purpose.

"It's good. Might spend my entire life trying to figure you out."

"What would you do when you do figure me out?"

"Not sure that will happen in my lifetime. Men can never figure out women."

Darcy snorted and rolled up on her side, giving her better reach of his body. "Men are the enigma. The gender that never makes sense. I don't understand them."

"Ask me a question. We're logical. We always make sense."

Darcy leaned over and licked his chest. "So, you say." She inched up his body and rubbed her face against his beard stubble. "Tell me about your tattoo. Why did you get it?"

"Ha. Leave it to you to pick out a non-logical action." He turned slightly to kiss her lips. They opened under his, allowing his tongue the entrance he wanted. They exchanged a long, leisurely kiss, lulling him into a drifting state between contentment and satiation.

"The cloverleaves, you never explained them."

Oh that, he'd almost forgotten with Darcy wrapped around him and exhaustion tugging at his muscles. "I wanted to be lucky."

"Don't all men?"

"Not get lucky. Be lucky. I was hardly past twenty-one, and I had no clue I was already lucky. Nothing bad had ever happened to me, yet. I went with a friend to dance revue audition. I had no intention of dancing, but they were short a man, and I was the right height to be the cop. My father carried a shield, although I'm betting he wasn't thrilled the first time I put on and took off a policeman's uniform." He chuckled trying to imagine his father's horrified expression.

"What does that have to do with the tattoo?" Darcy moved off him and pushed him slightly until he turned revealing the tattoo she had such an interest in. Her fingers outlined the edges. "It's very well done."

"Good thing too. It was part of our act."

"How so?" Her lips brushed over the tattoo.

"The nine of us all got together and wanted to do something to make our revue different. Plenty of men coming out in costumes from Indian chief to motorcycle cop. There were groups with men of different ethnic backgrounds and a few featured twins too. One night after a show, after one too many drinks, we all ended up at a tattoo shop. We all picked out different tattoos. Before the show began, we had the women fill out sheets, guessing what man had what tattoo. The winners got their own private dance with the dancer of their choice."

"I bet that was popular."

"It was."

"Did a lot of women guess yours?"

"Repeat customers did."

"Lot of those?"

"You'd be surprised."

"Not really."

HER PHONE CHIMED in the distance. Great. It stopped ringing, then started again. She strained her ears to listen. "It's my brother. What time is it, anyhow?"

Sometime during the night, Killian must have retrieved their clothes from the back deck. She shrugged on his discarded shirt and padded down the stairs to the living room. The raindrops on the tin roof explained the gray exterior. The phone started to ring again when she picked it up.

"Hello." The red time glowed 9:10.

"Darcy."

"Yes. William? Who did you expect?"

"You." His abrupt response indicated tension or irritation. "Are you in the cabin? Is Killian with you?"

"Yes. You gave him the key. Didn't you set up the cabin to be a romantic hideaway?"

"Elaine and I both did."

"Why the questions?" Did her brother want a play-by-play on how the night turned out? That type of behavior, she'd expect from Ruby.

"Killian's car blew up this morning."

Her heart skipped a beat. Surely, she heard wrong. *What would sound like car blew up? Threw, grew, drew?* "What?"

"The. Car. Blew. Up. Some type of explosion. Since it was left overnight in the town square, Joe Henry tried to tow it. He hooked it up, but when he started the truck, it blew. It mangled the truck's hook and jarred it enough that the truck's airbag deployed. Caused quite a disturbance."

"I imagine. Only reason Joe Henry hooked the car was to shake Killian down for money. He wouldn't have done that to a local."

"True." Her brother agreed. "A local would have broken into his compound lot and drove the vehicle home. All the same, despite his money-grubbing ways, I still feel for him. That explosion must have taken years off his life. Right now, Killian's aunt is beside herself. I told her I might know where he was. She said something about the people who shot him escaping from jail. She thinks they did it. His mother arrived in town too. I gave you as much time as I reasonably could, sis. You need to drive lover boy to town."

"I understand. He's not going to be a happy camper. I know I'm not. By the way, I appreciated the hot tub."

"Thought you would." He chuckled. "Oh no, Mrs. Blankenship, I'm not talking to your nephew."

Darcy sucked in a breath hearing Killian pad down the steps. She powered off the phone and gave a man a thorough stare, starting at his head, slipping over his very fine chest, his unbuttoned jeans and continuing to his bare toes.

"Ah, ready to go again. You are a tigress." He wrapped an arm around her waist and snugged her up to his side. "Who was on the phone?"

"My brother."

"Killjoy."

"You have no idea."

"What did he want?"

"Besides destroying my little bit of paradise. He wants me to drive you to town, now"

Killian's free hand rubbed over the bottom portion of his face. "Weird."

"It gets weirder."

His arm dropped from her waist as his eyebrows shot up. "Judging by your tone, I won't like whatever else you have to say."

Why does everything have to be so complicated? She already accepted that Killian was a cop and was about eighty percent okay with it. Her twenty percent uncertainty drowned in the hot tub. "Ah," she hesitated. "Your aunt is worried about you."

"Okay." He yawned, then grimaced slightly. "I am over twenty-one. Maybe I should have texted her to let her know I wasn't coming home last night. Did she ask your brother to call? How would she know where I was?"

"No, she didn't ask William to call. No, she doesn't know where you're at. It's possible she thinks you're dead."

"What the hell?" He patted down his pants pocket searching for his phone. "Did someone start a rumor that I died?"

"No, someone blew up your car."

"Not Leo? My car."

He named his car. She thought only women did that. "Yeah. Your aunt said something about the people you put behind bars escaping. She thinks they blew up the car and you with it. William volunteered to find you. Oh, and your mother is in town, too. We need to go before they send out a search party."

Killian took two steps backwards and felt behind him for the stairs. Once he located them, he slid down to a step and cradled his head. "Will this nightmare ever end?"

"Excuse me?" Darcy thought she knew what he was talking about, but she wanted to make sure.

His head came up slowly, and he regarded her with a weary expression. "I'm not talking about you or us. It's Heather and her gang of misfits. Sheer stupidity made me think she wanted me as opposed to narcotics sting information."

Even though she wanted to point out any woman would have been interested in him. She didn't. "Finish getting dressed. I'll do likewise."

"Yeah, will do. Wish I had my gun, though."

The thought Killian suspected he needed it chilled her a little. "Hey, I'm sure there is a non-criminal explanation for everything. Maybe there was a recall on your car."

"A car that explodes tends to make the news. As much as I hate to consider it, Heather has followed me to Monrovia. She asked about my entire family. At the time, I thought it showed interest. The wrong kind, I'm afraid. Maybe you should let me drive."

"No." She shook her head before dashing into the downstairs bathroom to tame her hair. She found a pair of purple sweats left behind from a previous visit that were a little tighter than she liked, but they'd do.

Killian stood by the door waiting when she poked her nose into the living room. She suspected he might have left if she hadn't taken the car keys with her. "All right, let's go meet the family."

Chapter Twenty

THIN SECTIONS OF pavement connected the pot holes, making driving a challenge even in the daylight. Darcy did her best to miss them, but her front tires might avoid one only to have a back wheel drop into a different one, catching for a second, causing Killian to swear. The man seethed beside her. She hadn't caused his anger, but it didn't make it any less unsettling.

What could she do to lighten up the atmosphere in the car? His constant checking the rearview mirror put her on edge. Maybe it was a cop thing, but it wasn't something he did the night before. Now that he knew certain criminals were out, he watched.

"The funniest thing happened to me the other day in the library." Her eyes cut right to Killian, who sat upright as if ready to spring from his seat as soon as she stopped. Even though her story wasn't that funny, she felt obligated to continue.

"This stranger wanders back into the stacks. Then my minister follows him. I'm on the other side of the shelves putting up books. The two of them start talking about an emerald heist."

Killian coughed and then gave her a disbelieving stare.

Well, at least he was listening. "The stranger had just got out of prison, and he wanted to know where the minister hid the emeralds."

"Are you making this up to distract me?"

"I'll admit to wanting to give you something else to think about rather than your family being in danger." Oh no, she did it again. "The men really were in the library and did talk about the emeralds. In fact, they were back again yesterday. Baldy, as I think of the stranger, pressed the minister for the jewel location. Anyhow, my minister said he'd call him with the info, which was weird since they both were standing there. Anyhow, last night when the bar was so crazy, I saw the minister and his wife come into the bar and sit down. Peculiar, since they never come to Sweaty's. I figured they were there either to have an alibi or prevent Baldy from going postal on them."

"You're telling me the truth?" The way he asked the question pretty much said he didn't believe her. Maybe he did hear some of the rumors around town.

"Yes, I am. In fact, I was worried for a while, convinced one of them saw me at the library, which explained my different outfits. I didn't want to be associated with the female in the white dress. Baldy kept coming into Sweaty's, and all he's said to me was a request for hot sauce or another beer, which means he didn't recognize me."

"Not necessarily, he could just be keeping an eye on you. Waiting to see what you might do, trying to decide if you know anything or even if you're a risk that should be taken out."

Her knuckles whitened on the steering wheel. "Thanks. I'd almost convinced myself I was being paranoid."

"Maybe you are. Could be the minister and the stranger have another type of relationship. Could be they're old *friends*."

Darcy tried to picture her staid minister having friends like Baldy, or even more bizarre having a romantic fling with the man. "Jewel thief is actually more believable, especially if it was a onetime thing."

"Hmm, did you tell anyone else?"

"I tried to tell your aunt, but she wouldn't listen. No one will listen to me." Before she could explain the town's general attitude, the sight of flashing lights caught her eyes. Monrovia didn't have their own force, so had to be the county mounty or state trooper on the scene. There were even red and white lights indicating a fire engine or an ambulance. Whatever it was brought the citizens out in droves.

Darcy steered her car in the direction of the town square. People lined the curb. Some even stood in the street. The smell of smoke hung in the air with the slight tinge of an electrical fire, probably due to all the computer gadgetry in the vehicle.

A teen pointed to her car. "There he is! He's alive."

Darcy felt like she was in a combination parade and walk of shame. "Hey, isn't that Darcy Darlington driving?" a woman yelled.

Too bad, she hadn't donned her sunglasses, but people would have recognized her car. Still, she tried to slide down in her seat as she parked near the state trooper car. Killian swung the car door open before she'd even shifted into park.

"Mom!" He embraced a concerned looking woman clutching a small dog.

The woman returned the hug with one arm until the dog protested with ear-piercing yips. "Sorry. Gigi isn't a hugger. Thank goodness, you're okay. Monica practically broke the sound barrier to get here after Leticia told me you were missing along with your car exploding. Monica is around here somewhere?" She turned her head side to side, searching.

The open car door provided the perfect opportunity to eavesdrop. Maybe she should get out and introduce herself. Yeah, that's what she'd do. Darcy slid out of the car, wondering what she would say to the mother of the man who had her screaming in ecstasy most of the night. Something besides a hearty thank you might be more appropriate. Nothing was coming to mind,

A tall slender redhead wearing a dog rescue shirt joined mother and son. "Look, Monica. Killian's alive!"

It made sense his mother would be excited, but why would Monica. The woman gave him an uncertain smile. Ah, then it hit her. This was Mama's choice.

"Monica, meet my son, Killian."

He held his hand out to the woman who gave it a weak shake. Darcy felt awkward and glanced around for an open business she could pretend to visit. There was the post office about two blocks up. Stamps, she needed stamps. Might as well take her purse to make it look authentic.

"Darcy, where are you going?" Killian called after her. "I want you to meet my mother."

"Ah, yes." She changed direction, not knowing how to handle what would have to be an awkward situation. "Hello." She held out her hand to the woman who gave her a measuring look. At first, she would have thought there wasn't any of Leticia in this woman, but they both managed the same stare down. The woman gave her hand a firm shake before going for the jugular.

"How do you know my son?"

Killian moved closer and waved his hand in front of his mother. "This is the woman who saved my life. If it wasn't for her I'd be dead now."

In the distance, her brother William escorted Leticia Blankenship their way. The woman had her arm tucked in her brother's crooked arm as if they were posing for junior prom photos. It would serve Darcy well to leave before they arrived.

"It was nothing. Well, got to go." She did a slight sliding step, one she learned in line dancing, but Killian kept on talking, delaying her exit.

"If it hadn't been for Darcy, I'd be in the car when the bomb went off."

Leticia answered before his mother did. "Oh, please, she probably rigged up that bomb herself to trick your son into falling into her arms."

If she'd felt judged before, being the center of several pairs of eyes made it even more awkward. How could she make a graceful getaway? Maybe her brother would save her. Ha! He laughed. Her brother laughed. His face grew red as he continued to chuckle. William even let go of Leticia's arm to bend forward and rest his hands on his knees as he gasped for air. Finally, he straightened, nodded in her direction. As a good brother, he'd have to say something about her sterling character.

"Darcy could never make a bomb. She couldn't even pass chemistry. Our father made me let her copy my homework."

There was a collective intake of air that should have sucked in the city block. Thanks a lot, brother.

"Oh, come on." She held out her open hands to the crowd. "Not one of you ever copied homework." No one admitted to it, even though the odds were against most passing chemistry on their own merits.

Leticia shook her finger in her direction. "A cheat and a liar."

"Not a bomb maker," William added.

Could it get any worse? Even Monica gave her the evil eye as if she knew what she and Killian had been up to last night and this morning.

"That's no way to talk about the woman I love." Killian wrapped an arm around her and dropped a kiss on her hair.

His casually delivered comment made Darcy doubt its validity, but Monica's open mouth and Leticia's gasp of horror reflected their perceptions all too well. What would be so wrong with Killian falling for her? The acrid smell of motor fuel and electrical components reminded her of the reason they'd left their hideaway.

"Your car." She turned to stare at the twisted hunk of metal minus two doors and a windshield. The thousand pound plus hook on the tow trunk looked more like crumpled tin foil than a solid metal. At least the tow driver survived and currently leaned against the ambulance holding a cold pack against his nose. No way Killian would have. His mother must have the same thought because she launched herself at Darcy with a sob.

"Thank goodness he was with you." She murmured the words into Darcy's neck along with a little slobber and snot.

"Ah." Awkward pause and she had no clue what to say or if it would be okay to wipe off the dampness Killian's mother left behind. "Well, me too." It didn't sound exactly like a reply, but maybe his mom didn't notice since she was still hanging on to her.

"That Heather," Killian's mother breathed the words into Darcy's ear, "I never trusted her. Figured she was just another skank. My son tends to prefer those types."

"Mother," Killian's voice was firm as he wrapped his hands around his mother's wrists trying to undo his mother's firm grasp on Darcy. "We, um, don't need to talk about this right now."

She released her grip on Darcy's arm and gave her son a distracted smile. "Right now, we need to track down the scheming bitch who blew up your car. I brought my pistol."

Chapter Twenty-One

T HE SOUNDS OF voices debating against the inadvisability of tracking Heather down faded as Darcy stepped away from the group. Most of the locals were drifting away as the firemen rolled up their hose. She circled the blackened hulk of the car, imagining how the evening could have turned out differently. Water dripped down onto the colored foam that flowed around the chassis. The firemen probably hit it with the foam first.

Thinking how easily it could be her, her fingers grazed the blackened metal. Most women would have jumped at the chance to ride in Killian's car. Most people probably thought she would. A movement in the shadows caught her eyes. Baldy, her visiting felon, threw her an enigmatic glance before vanishing,

What if… she almost didn't want to consider it… if the explosion was more about her than Killian? He'd just be collateral damage. Heather and her crew did manage to escape. If not the whole gang, at least part of it. With an officer shot and killed, the minimum they'd get would be life. Anyone with sense would hightail it out of the state, possibly the country.

Ronny had his hands in his pockets, and his John Deere hat pushed back on his head as he strolled over to her. "Honey of a car. Not right that someone would treat it that way."

"No, it stinks." She wrinkled her nose, thinking more about the woman who'd pretended to care for Killian to feed her drug buddies information. Did she ever care about him, even a little?

"Yeah." Ronny jingled his truck keys and his change. "City folks live in the fast lane. People get hurt. You could have been in the car."

"I've considered it."

"I bet you have." He reached out to grab her arm. "I know now isn't the best time, but I'll take you back. Even though," He angled his head in Killian's direction, "you and he bumped uglies."

Not the most romantic description she ever heard, especially with the uglies part. "You're right. It's not a good time." A hard jerk dislodged his hand as she walked in the direction of the buildings.

Ronny called after her. "At least, no one blew up my truck."

She wanted to tell him that was because no one would believe she'd be with him, but she didn't. She couldn't even get to her car because everyone she didn't want to see lingered around it. The back door might be open to Sweaty's. Even though it wasn't open for business they had deliveries in the morning. Inside, she'd call Ruby or possibly her mother. Either one would give her a ride home.

William would do her the courtesy of driving her car home. She'd have to decide on what to do next. Her library job exploded along with the car. If the explosion was meant for her, then it would be best if she reinvented herself somewhere else. Might as well forget about Killian after his mother labeled his romantic interests skanks. Rather than argue the label, it might be better to not say anything. As for the kiss on the head, it could be nothing more than gratitude for not being dead.

Her shoulders hunched forward as her gaze dropped to the ground. The various cracks, stains, and holes served as a road map of sorts. The tumbled bricks announced the back of the hardware store that shut its doors more than a decade ago. No one ever expressed an interest in taking over the empty store. Not too surprising since businesses left

Monrovia without any new ones on the horizon. Some locals were quick to point the fingers at those who drove to the next town to shop at their discount mart, but Darcy had spotted most of the citizens there at one time or another.

Just the other day they had pretty lace trimmed bra with matching panties for under sixteen dollars. A bargain like that was hard to resist. Maybe she should have gotten the teal set instead of the peach one. Peach was more for blondes or redheads. When she relocated, she'd dye her hair. Yeah, things would be different when she moved. A name change would be needed, something unremarkable. Should she go with a current name like Stephanie or an older one such as Mary?

A footfall interrupted her musings, but before she could react a sweat saturated fabric dropped over her head the same time an arm tightened across her windpipe choking her. Darcy kicked out, hitting something solid.

"Ow. The bitch kicked me."

"That's not all I'll do." She managed to force the words out despite the strong arm against her throat making it hard to breathe.

"Shut her up!" A nearby woman snapped.

The unfamiliar voice surprised her as the arm across her neck made it increasingly difficult to breathe. Darcy tried to pull in air through her nose without success. What was happening? Why would there be a woman giving orders? The pastor's wife didn't have the ruthless bone in her body. No way, she'd head up some felonious gang.

"What are we going to do with her?"

The voice sounded near her ear as she was prodding into walking. Even though she couldn't see, Darcy knew this stretch of the alley. Before she started working at Sweaty's, she used the narrow strip behind the building as a shortcut between the high school and the drugstore that served as her go to spot for an after-school snack. The soured milk smell indicated they were close to the sports bar. Why

Clyde even ordered milk surprised her. No one had ever ordered it in the time she'd worked there.

She needed to leave a trail. Her one arm was bent painfully behind her. Her left arm pressed uselessly against her side. She tried to brush her hand upward, but only caught the edge of her jacket.

Something furry touched her hand. The rabbit's foot William had given her when they both turned ten. It had been his favorite charm, but even at that young age her brother realized she needed luck more than he did. Darcy had kept it for years, transferring it from her backpack to her jacket. The years took its toll on the clip, forcing Darcy to attach the foot with tape, a flimsy stopgap measure.

Her foot caught on something, forcing a stumble, Darcy drooped against her captor, surprising him. The fabric slipped, allowing her a glimpse of a bearded man. She didn't know him, which made her wonder why he'd kidnap her.

The man reached for her the same time the woman shoved a gun in her face.

"Don't make a sound or it will be the last one you make."

The glacial blue eyes carried a certainty that kept Darcy's lips sealed. She didn't need a neon sign to know the blonde's deadly intentions. Many a man would have been taken in by her looks, not caring that the beauty could be dangerous. Her hand tightened on the rabbit's foot. She jerked downward, pulling it free and dropped it to the ground. She kept her eyes on the woman as she nodded.

"Good. We understand each other. We'll make better time without the jacket over your head. Let's go."

An upward jerk had her standing and her arm almost out of socket. The three of them stumbled past Sweaty's closed door, the alley funneled sound from the departing fire engine and ambulance.

People should be leaving. Maybe even a few might use the alley as a short cut. Unfortunately, the same thought must have occurred to her captors. "We need to hurry." The man's voice broke betraying nervousness. "Not sure why we had to come to this one-horse town anyhow. It should be enough to escape."

His companion waved her gun as she jogged beside him. "No one asked you. Keep in mind if it wasn't for me there wouldn't have been an escape. You would still be in jail with your buddy."

The man grunted, twisting Darcy's arm as they jogged near the end of the alley. Running did make him release his chokehold some. The nose of a white panel van stuck out near the end of the alley. A hasty spray paint job covered writing. A plumber or painter probably walked out of their home this morning and wondered what happened to his van.

Really, a white van, the accepted vehicle of all criminals, and no one noticed it?

The woman sprinted for the van, pulling out a set of keys as she ran. Maybe they hadn't stolen it. "Tie up and stifle the slut," she ordered.

What was this insult Darcy day? The back door popped open courtesy of the woman. Both her captors muscled her in as she kicked out and managed a short scream. She cupped her fingers and clawed at the woman's face, only realizing at the last moment that super short nails wouldn't do any damage. A knee in her back pinned her to the floor while duct tape wrapped around her mouth and head, embedding in her hair.

Had anyone heard her? Was her scream as puny as it sounded? If they taped her hands, all she'd have to do was bring them up over her head to break the duct tape bond. She'd read about the technique in a magazine about women's self-defense.

Bearded guy must have read the magazine. He pulled her arms behind her. Great. *Someone save her from smart kidnappers. Why even kidnap me? It wasn't like anyone would pay to get me back.*

Once he wrapped her ankles several times with duct tape, Bearded One left her on the floor like a sack of kitty litter. Darcy stared at the various tools secured to the walls and boxes of supplies. It was a work van for possibly some home repairman, or even a carpenter. The one thing a carpenter always had besides a hammer and a measuring tape, would be a saw.

The van made a few short turns as it headed out of town. *Okay, nosy citizens, isn't anyone noticing an unfamiliar van speeding out of town?*

"Heather, I don't understand why we took the girl."

Darcy held her head off the carpet. She wanted to know why they grabbed her, too.

"The mother would have been better. My goal is to hurt Killian. The cop is way too lucky for his own good. He should be dead twice over by now."

Ah, that explained her kidnapping. Well, sort of.

"The girl, though. You always said the man was a cold one since he never warmed up to you."

Heather spat inside the van before answering. "He didn't appreciate quality. Last night, when we went in that sports bar, he didn't even notice us. His eyes were on her. When he wasn't leering at her, he glared at any man who even looked at her. He never looked at me that way. If he had, I probably wouldn't have shot his partner, thinking the man was him. It's never good to leave loose ends."

Darcy didn't have to be a mind reader to realize she was now a loose end. If Bearded One gave it much thought, he'd realize he was one too.

"So, what's our plan? Are we going to get money for the chick?"

A cramp was forming in her neck from keeping her head off the floor.

"Nope."

Just as she thought. Darcy rested her cheek on the floor as she scanned the walls for sharp, pointy objects.

"Why take her?"

Yeah, Heather, what's the deal? I never had anything to do with you and your drug operation.

"I want to pay back Killian for the way he treated me."

"The part where he let you live with him rent free and provided information about which houses to rob?"

"No!" she screamed, accompanied by a thud.

The van swerved, causing Darcy to hit the wall. Something tumbled from a shelf and hit her.

"You didn't have to hit me. The cop should be pissed. You used him, killed his partner, and probably destroyed his career. He might even go to prison."

As curious as Darcy was about the woman's motivation, the slim metal strip resting across her face interested her more. It was a blade from a hacksaw. If only she could somehow get the blade back to her hands.

"The man locked us both up. He knew enough to track us down. That should be reason enough to blow him up."

"Don't get your panties in a wad. I hear you, but the man was doing his job. I think this is something else. You told me it was a job, but I think you had the hots for him."

Well, gee, Einstein, she was living with him.

They had to keep arguing and driving as she worked her way to the blade. If she could roll over, which was no problem and work her way up about a foot and half, it should be within finger range. Although without a handle, it would be difficult to maneuver the jagged edge.

"I had to sleep with him, or it would have been weird."

Darcy grimaced, not liking the mental image. She managed a barrel roll, trapping the blade behind her back.

"Did you hear something?" the man asked, forcing Darcy to close her eyes. If he thought she was asleep, perhaps, he'd not consider her up to anything as nefarious as survival. "Guess it is just stuff rolling around in the back. The female is out."

"Damn. These small-town girls have no guts. She probably fainted, overwhelmed by everything. If I knew that was the type of thing Killian liked, I could have pulled that act."

"Why do you care what he liked or didn't like? He was a tool to be used. Any other narcotics officer would have served."

"Yeah, but none of them were as sexy. He certainly was nice to look at. The man could even be kind. He fixed dinner more than once."

I don't really want to hear this. I'd agree Killian is a sweetheart, but I rather think he saves that aspect of himself for me and not every stacked criminal who stumbles across his path.

Her finger tips touched the rough metal blade, debating how to saw the tape. Her hands were facing each other, which was a plus. She bent her wrists until the blade rested against the edge of the tape. A slight rocking motion with her wrists could create some breakage as the blade cut into the tape. Ah, she needed was a cut to pull the rest of it apart.

"Just as I thought. No wonder you let it play out so long. I told Raoul you were taking chances. The longer you took the more possibility of us getting caught."

"Without me you would have never known about the sting, and everyone would have been caught. There would have been no one to spring us."

"Yeah, I'm glad to be out and all, but doesn't that make you wonder how easy we escaped."

Darcy stopped in mid-saw. Hey, she hadn't considered it since her energy focused on survival.

"Police can be lazy. You forget I can be very persuasive." She purred the last word.

"Most of your persuasion involves a loaded gun and the occasional knife. The sooner we go to ground the better I'd feel. You never answered me about the female."

"Ah, her."

Yes, her. Darcy didn't dare open her eyes or hold her head up just in case they glanced back to judge if she was listening.

"I'll call Killian. Tell him I have her. Ask for money."

"You said we weren't getting money."

"I know. This will keep him busy and give him hope. We'll just shoot the woman and drop her in a ditch so the cops will find her fast."

Chapter Twenty-Two

A T LAST, THE townspeople shuffled back to their homes giving the charred hunk of twisted metal a backward glance. Killian waved as his mother, aunt, and Monica climbed into a car with Darcy's mother and brother. The two of them insisted on taking the women home and feeding them breakfast. William had invited him, but he promised to join them later, after he located Darcy.

The woman vanished during the chaos, but he assumed it was about the time Monica showed or his mother mentioned his habit of associating with skanks. Family sure made it hard to have a love life.

The trio of elderly male gossips from the gas station huddled on the corner by a lamppost. He held up a hand in greeting. "Hey, I was wondering if you could help me. Did any of you see Darcy Darlington zip by?"

Instead of answering, they nudged one another and laughed. One gave him a broad wink. "Can't keep track of your women, huh?"

Irritation needled him, making him want to bark a reply, but he knew better. He managed a slight smile. "There's only one woman for me. I think she might be playing hard to get. Misunderstanding, you know how women can be."

Another round of laughter and nudging, before one angled his head toward the alley.

Squealing tires announced the approach of a vehicle, one moving fast. A black and white police car careened down the street and slammed on the brakes beside him. Killian jumped sideways, back onto the sidewalk to avoid getting hit. A close look identified his sergeant driving. The man swung open the door. "We need to talk."

Killian gestured to the burnt-out hulk of his car. "I got the message that Heather and her crew are free. How could you let that happen?"

"About that, there's something you need to know."

Killian turned away, and made his way between the buildings, uninterested in why the guards failed to make appropriate precautions for dangerous prisoners. Right now, all he wanted to do was find Darcy and explain things, such as his mother and her relentless attempts to fix him up.

The sergeant swung out his car and shadowed Killian. "I know you're pissed about everything, but I'm still your boss. As your boss, you need to stop and listen."

Killian knew he should stop, especially since he hadn't decided just yet if he wanted to give up the force. It wouldn't be smart to anger the man who believed in him. A blue furry object caught his attention. He picked it up and turned it over. It reminded him of the one from Darcy's jacket. He held it up to his nose. It carried the stale odor of onions and frying hamburgers. Definitely hers. The ragged tape indicated it was torn off, which made him wonder why. He tucked the charm into his pocket to give to her once he found her.

"Did you hear anything I said?" the winded man inquired.

Killian hadn't, he noticed a few years behind the desk tended to make a man go soft. "Say again?"

"We let them escape, intentionally."

"What the hell! You do know they blew up my car, and I could have been driving it."

Sergeant Boswick slapped his chest. "Yeah, I heard. Trust me, that wasn't my plan. I thought they'd lead us to the big guys in the distribution ring. They were small fish. Figured they'd go running back with their tails between their legs. They still might, but it looks like they had a vendetta to settle with you first."

"I noticed that. I'm worried about my relatives. I'd appreciate if a patrol car would keep watch on my mother's house."

"It's already done, but keeping your mother in one place is another issue. I have roadblocks up in a fifty-mile radius to catch them."

Killian stuck his hand into his pocket and fingered the soft rabbit's foot as he conversed. "Good plan, but this is country. They could leave the road, cut through a cornfield, hide out in an abandoned barn. There's a million possibilities. Not much, I can do about it since I'm on suspension," he said, even though right now, finding Darcy served as his number one priority,

"About that," Boswick slapped him on the back and continued, "You're back on the force. I brought your gun and shield."

The words he'd been waiting to hear should have excited him more than they did. An uneasy sense of apprehension tugged at him. The car exploding may have been the first shoe to hit the floor, and there was always a second. "That's good?"

He ignored his sergeant's affronted look as he thought aloud. "Heather would have heard by now that I wasn't in the car. I wouldn't put it past her to stick around just to watch it blow up. I suspect she's still in town. Did you bring a photo of her?"

"In the car."

"Let's go get it." The two of them retrieved the photo. Killian knew just who to ask. The gossip squad was still at the lamppost. They hadn't made their way to the gas station yet. He held out Heather's mug shot, which didn't do her justice since she'd snarled for the camera.

"Have you seen this woman?"

They passed the photo around. One held it at arm's length and squinted at it. "You think that's her, the one with the bearded guy? The same ones who went into the alley after Darcy?"

His stomach dropped. The casual words painted images he didn't care to examine.

"Yep. That's her. Only she was smiling when I saw her."

The thought of harming the only woman he truly cared about would make Heather smile. His hands fisted by his side. In the shootout, he could have killed Heather, but that wasn't who he was. Even though people thought police shot to kill, they didn't. They shot to disable—if possible. A wounded criminal could be a goldmine of information.

The police car radio squawked, forcing the sergeant to duck into the car listen. He called out to Killian. "What happened to your cell phone?"

"Good question. I had it last night in my car. Why?"

"Looks like Heather has your girlfriend. When she couldn't reach you, she called your mother."

"Fuck."

"Exactly. Do you think your girlfriend has her phone on her?"

"I don't know. Possibly."

"We can track her using her phone GPS."

"Maybe Heather will call again."

"I doubt it."

He did too, knowing being denied the ability to make him squirm would result in Heather taking it out on Darcy. If she called his phone, he would have been able to initiate an immediate trace, but his phone went up in flames with the car.

Anger wrestled with helplessness as he turned over the possible scenario in his mind. Darcy left due to the awkwardness of meeting his mother and potential girlfriend. Heather followed her. The woman had a nose for sniffing out weaknesses and identified Darcy as his.

Instead of following her as he should have, he attempted to calm his volatile relatives. They did think he died a fiery death, after all. William assured him Darcy was fine, but Killian knew better. Why have instincts if you ignore them? As if on cue, a mental spark flared. He gestured to his sergeant. "Small towns have no police departments, but they do have their own town watchmen."

He nodded at the three men who regarded him with undisguised interest.

"Something wrong with Darcy?"

Killian cleared his throat. "Something is very wrong. Strangers, the same ones, who blew up my car and wrecked the tow truck, may have kidnapped her."

The three of them gave a unified gasp and looked at one another. The one with the Red Man Cap spat a tobacco stream on the ground. "See, I told you those two were up to no good. We should have followed them."

"Couldn't stand it if anything happened to Darcy. She's the only person that keeps the town from being flat out boring. Gotta love her spunk."

The third man nodded and added, "Just the other day when her car ran out of gas…"

Killian held up his hand before they could start any more Darcy stories. "Have you seen any unfamiliar vehicles in town?"

One man pointed to the police car.

"Besides that."

"How about that burgundy sedan?"

"That was my mother's car."

The three of them looked at each other, just when he thought they'd say nothing. One cleared this throat. "Remember that white van? I pointed it out to you because someone did a bad job spray painting white paint over the words. You could still read Handyman

Services."

The other two men agreed. "It had New Jersey plates, too. It's the type of thing I'd expect from someone from New Jersey."

Before the man even completed his sentence, the sergeant called it in.

"At least, we know what to look for," his sergeant confirmed. "Now, we wait."

Waiting wasn't good enough. "I need my gun and shield."

"Don't go off half-cocked."

"I'm not waiting." Killian returned to his observant trio for information. "Any good places to hide out around here?"

"There's Farmer Jones' old silo. It's off County Road 40."

"Ignore Tuck, he's not thinking. No city folks would know the silo is abandoned. There's a barn on 200N that is halfway tumbled down. It was a tobacco shed, out in the field, not that close to anything. There's an access road that lead to it, too. McCormicks haven't raised tobacco in years."

Killian wrote down all the possibilities. His head went up as he realized a very major obstacle. "Shit, I have no car."

His sergeant nudged him. "I'm here."

THE TIRES HUMMING on the pavement alerted Darcy. The van had picked up speed and no longer had to putt around pretending to be a type of service vehicle. The idea of an outsider would inspire suspicion since people worked on their own homes, cleaned their own carpets using the rental cleaner from the IGA, and a non-functioning vehicle served as a reason for two or more men to gather around an open hood usually with a beer in one hand. In other words, there'd be no need for a service van.

Her fingers cramped around the blade as she continued her upward rocking motion. Sometimes the metal teeth snagged the duct tape. Other times, it completely missed it. Darcy pulled her wrist apart about an eighth of an inch. Her top teeth settled on her bottom lip as a pain rippled through her hands and up her arms.

"We should off her here or close by." Heather suggested casually as if talking about a picnic, providing the motivation Darcy needed to continue to saw through the pain.

How could Killian even spend one minute with the cold-blooded woman? Still, the way Killian told his version of the Heather tale, he never asked her to live with him out of a great love. No, the woman showed up with a sad tale of not being able to afford her apartment after her roommate moved out.

Her nostrils flared as she fought the response to snort at such a flimsy excuse. Men could be taken in so easily. Then again, Heather had the shapely figure and blonde tresses that most men fantasize about. *Really, brain, you had to go there on me? Last thought before death would have to be something about how hot Killian found Heather.*

"I don't know about doing it here. Someone might find her right away." The man shifted in his seat, and his voice became fainter as if he changed direction while speaking. "Someone might find us."

The man's caution worked for Darcy since she hadn't freed herself yet. Never mind, she hadn't worked her way to step two where she secured a weapon capable of defending herself against a bullet. In the end, it would be two against one.

Various tools hung on the walls, including what could be shears, a sledge hammer, and crowbar. The sledgehammer had promise, but only if she could throw it around like Thor. Something spectacular such as a flamethrower would work. It would give her the element of surprise. The ability to shapeshift into a dangerous creature would work, too. Wait a minute, as a pissed off female, she happened to be one of the most feared beings in the male world. Now, all she had to do was convince Heather's lackey that it'd be preferable to be on her side as opposed to his lethal leader's.

"I want her to be found. Better yet, I could gut shot her, assuring her death, but just long enough for her to be found and relay to Killian, or whoever finds her, that her brutal death was all Killian's fault."

No way would I say that.

"She wouldn't say that."

At least, the man had more smarts than I originally thought.

"She would if I told her to."

"No, she wouldn't, especially if you already shot her. She'd have nothing to lose."

Darcy moved her fingers faster, aware that the murderous leader might not be working with a full deck. Could be she never had a complete set.

Her lips twisted as gave the bonds another test. The tape moved a little more. Good, but not good enough. She had to free both her wrists and ankles, and then it might be better to escape while the van was in motion by rolling out the back. She might not survive the fall, but it was better than the alternative.

"We could pin a note to her. Something like this death was brought to you by Officer Killian…"

"Are you fucking kidding me? My mistake was coming back with you. I should have known better than to trust you, but I ignored your cop obsession if it got me free."

"Why you!"

Darcy watched as if in slow motion as Heather lifted her gun in the direction of the passenger seat. A shot rang out, maybe two, it was hard to tell with the chaos. The van lurched off the road. The uneven ground threw the still bound Darcy between the two walls studded with heavy metal tools and stopped as the vehicle slammed into something. Darcy flew into a van wall with one final hard jolt. The airbags deployed with a hiss spewing white powder everywhere.

Not the ending, she expected, but it worked. Darcy managed to roll to the middle of the van a second before the sledgehammer fell. Her heart stopped with the realization. It would be a shame to have survived a kidnapping only to have her life snuffed out by an errant tool.

A close encounter with death had her gasping for air, which was difficult with her taped mouth. Panic would have to wait until she escaped. Her cell vibrated in her pocket. She had the means of rescue all the time. All she had to do was get her hands free.

Chapter Twenty-Three

THE CELL GPS led Killian to a little used county road. Just the type of place a killer might pick for a body dump. Steam wafted from the white van wrapped around a tree. Oh no, he was too late. He swung open the door even before the vehicle came to a full stop.

"Wait." His sergeant called out. "You could be walking into a trap."

The words stopped his forward motion as effectively as an ice wall. Yeah, that would be a stupid move. He could be gunned down before he could help Darcy. He squeezed his eyes shut and took a deep breath. Put away the emotion. Use logic. Where might Heather and crew be hiding? Spindly pines and broader hardwoods grew sporadically near the road and huddled closer together in the distance. Wherever they were, they probably had a bead on him.

Killian stood motionless in midstride resembling a yoga devotee demonstrating the second warrior pose if it included a gun. A sound erupted from near the van. His eyes cut to that direction while he slowly moved into position and gestured for his sergeant.

A rumpled Darcy with a wide strip of duct tape tangled with her tresses came around the van, shaking a cell phone. "It shows two bars, but no service."

"Are you okay?" He couldn't believe his eyes. Here he was supposed to be the hero riding to the rescue. Somehow, the woman managed to get free on her own.

Her head jerked up. "Killian!" She yelled his name as she launched herself into his arms.

The five-second warning gave him enough time to holster his gun. His arms enveloped her and pulled her tight. He closed his eyes. "Thank God, you're okay. I'm not sure what I would do if anything happened to you."

Darcy squeezed him back. "I almost believe you."

"You should."

A throat clearing reminded him that they weren't alone and he was still on duty. He dropped his arms and took a step back. He managed an apologetic grin before starting his inquiry. "What happen to your kidnappers? I assume you were abducted?"

"I was. Something about Heather wanting to make you squirm. In the end, she planned on having you jump through hoops to get me back. Joke would be on you since she planned on killing me first."

Forget being official. He tangled his fingers with Darcy. "I'm so sorry. You didn't deserve this. It's my fault."

"Not really. Heather was going to do what she was going to do. We both were obstacles in her path."

His thumb smoothed a circular path on her open palm. "I should have protected you, not pulled you into the mess."

Sergeant Boswick coughed. "Okay. Everyone is glad to see each other. Need to know where your abductors are."

"Dead." Darcy answered casually as she pulled a strand of hair from its duct tape restraint.

That would explain why Darcy was free, although it was hard to imagine her taking on both of them.

"Did the wreck kill them?" Boswick gestured to the van.

Darcy took a couple steps closer to the crumpled front end of the van. "Wow, that's bad. Never really looked at the damage until now.

Too busy unwrapping myself and trying to get cell service. If they had been alive, the crash might have killed them."

Boswick shot him an irritated look, which was easy enough to interpret. He needed to get information from Darcy. "How did they die?"

"Well, I was laying all the floor of the van trussed up like a Thanksgiving turkey while they argued about where to kill me. Then they started yelling about something else. Not totally sure, it may have been how their plans were going. Heather pulled out her gun and shot her guy. It must have been the same time he shot her. The van jumped the road and crashed."

Killian stepped closer and wrapped an arm around her. "Are you sure you're all right after being thrown around in van hurtling itself into the trees?"

"I'm good. Sure, I'll have a few bruises, but at least I wasn't brained by the sledgehammer."

He wasn't sure what she meant, but he'd insist on a medical exam just to be sure. Shock often hit later. Darcy slumped against him. His arms wrapped around her to prevent her from hitting the ground.

The sergeant spoke into his shoulder mounted radio. "Send another ambulance." He nodded at Killian. "Surprised, she lasted as long as she did."

A SENSE OF urgency caused Darcy to thrash against her restraints and murmur. "No, no, I don't know anything. I didn't see anything." Instinct shouted to run, but she needed to see where she was going first. A dark-eyed woman with a stethoscope wrapped around her neck leaned over her.

"You're safe now."

"There's no jewel thieves."

"Huh?" The woman blinked. "I was told you'd been kidnapped by felons who were holding you hostage. No one told me anything about jewel thieves."

Memories of her recent harrowing ride in the van returned. "Ah, it must have been a dream." As soon as she could, she needed to impress on Killian the present danger of Baldy. With the recent upheaval, the man made have left town or decided to hunker down until everything settled again.

"Ah, you need better dreams than that, especially with such a handsome man worried about you."

She left William behind in town, so the medic had to be talking about Killian. "Yeah, I do have better things to think about." Make that after the jewel thieves were picked up. She tried to sit up, but the restraints kept her flat against the gurney.

"Is this really necessary?" A finger of anxiety stroked her neck. Second time today she couldn't move her arms. She wiggled against the straps, hoping to make her point evident.

"Love to help you." The ambulance made an abrupt left turn throwing the medic across the space. She grabbed the overhead panic bar to prevent herself from bumping into the side. "As you can see, you have the safest seat in the house. Once we get there and the transfer is made, you will be able to sit up. Hang on a few more minutes."

Considering all she'd been through sitting tight, make that lying tight, for a little longer wasn't much. The scream of a siren blew past them, making her realize the lack of one. "The siren, not us?" She knew the answer as the sound faded into the distance.

"Nope. You're going in at regular speed since you aren't in cardiac arrest or bleeding out. Technically, they could have buckled you in the police car and got you there faster, but your boyfriend wanted you to have the best care."

"He's not my boyfriend." Darcy protested the medic's point, not certain if what she and Killian had was a relationship. Would she even want a romance with a cop if it involved kidnapping by vindictive felons?

"Please." The woman wrinkled her nose. She kept one hand wrapped around the bar while she gestured with her free one. "As an emergency care medic, I get calls all the time from panicked husbands or boyfriends. It's always easy to tell the ones who care."

"How?" It made her wonder what Killian did to demonstrate boy-friend material.

"The ones who care usually ask to ride in the ambulance. Of course, they can't. When I tell them that, they give me a brief medical history and instructions to tell their loved one that they love them."

"Ah, what did Killian say?"

The woman laughed. "I'd knew you'd ask. He told me you wouldn't like being restrained. Tell the folks at the hospital not to cut the duct tape out of your hair. He'd get a bottle of mineral oil and clean off the duct tape himself. Now, that's love."

Her lips twisted to one side. Doubt anyone else would want to separate her hair from the sticky tape. "If I play my cards right, I might even get a shampoo out of it."

"Ooh romantic." The medic placed her hand over heart. "So, where did you meet such a prime male?"

"Outside the library, while I was being hassled by another guy."

"He rode to your rescue?"

"Eventually."

"Your story keeps getting better and better. I need stories like yours. Right now, I'm in a romance free zone due to a divorce. Stories like yours give me hope."

"Not sure if I gave anyone hope before."

"You might be surprised."

The ambulance turned into the emergency entrance and gave a

short siren shriek as it stopped. The back door swung open and hands guided the gurney down onto the pavement and into the red glow of the emergency sign. No sooner had the twin entry doors swung closed behind her than she heard Killian's voice.

"Where's Darcy Darlington?"

Twenty minutes after her initial entry, a flustered Killian entered her cubicle. "There's a real pit bull nurse out there who wasn't going to let me back here."

"Imagine that. I see you managed to get in."

"It wasn't easy. I called your mother and explained what happened. I even gave the phone to Miss You Shall Not Pass. Apparently, your mother didn't sound convincing. She pointed out I could call up anyone with instructions for her to pretend to be my mother." He worked his way around the bed to grab the hand without the IV in it.

"I'm sure the woman was only doing her job."

He huffed slightly. "Your mother is on her way. I may not have explained the entire situation since I wanted her to drive safe."

"Wise. You have a better handle on my family than I do. So, how did you get past the nurse?"

"I had to flash my badge and tell her I was here to take your official statement."

"She believed you after your previous attempts?"

"Not really. I had to show my driver's license, too."

She chuckled imagining Killian foiled by the no nonsense nurse. "Well, you're here now. Want my statement?"

Killian pulled a small tape recorder out of his pocket. "I'll record this so I won't end up asking you to repeat things."

She was almost done with her statement when her mother, brother, and Elaine rushed in. Her mother sprinted past her brother in a burst of speed.

"Baby girl, what's this I hear about kidnapping?"

Darcy checked out Killian, who held his hands out and shrugged his shoulders. "Who told you?"

"Grandpa Willie."

Killian's eyebrows went up.

Darcy explained. "You met him in front of the gas station. He's part of the town gossip squad."

"Ah, him." He held one finger. "The man was instrumental in finding you. He knew there was an unfamiliar van in town and that it had Jersey tags. He told me to find you because the town wouldn't be fun without you in it."

"Forget about it being the right thing to do. Still, it is somewhat flattering that I make the town fun."

Elaine stood by her feet and gave her blanket-covered legs a pat. "He's not the only one."

Two people almost made a fan club. She grinned at the group. "Who knows, I may have to think of something else to enliven the town."

Her mother pressed her hand against her heart. "Please don't."

Chapter Twenty-Four

A WEEK LATER, Killian and Darcy strolled through downtown Monrovia. A black greasy spot denoted where the charger burned to a crisp. Darcy couldn't look at the spot without shuddering.

"A few good rains should get rid of it," Killian told her.

"Possibly. So, when are you headed back to the city?" She tried to make her words sound casual as if she didn't have that much riding on his answer.

"Well," he hesitated and squeezed her hand. "I did want to talk to you about that. This recent incident, my partner killed, you kidnapped, and my car exploding has made me consider a quieter way of life."

"What do you mean?" Even though they kept strolling, her breath caught as she waited for his answer. No way she could hold her breath indefinitely and keep moving.

"I decided to try something different." They reached the abandoned hardware store when Killian pulled keys out of his pocket and flourished them. "How about humoring me and peeking inside?"

"All right." Her curiosity aroused by his unusual actions. The wide windows allowed in bright sunlight highlighting the dust motes dancing in the air. A musty odor of disuse rode the air. Their footprints made impressions on the dusty floor exposing the wood flooring. "So, you have the key, why?"

She dropped his hand and turned in a slow circle, taking in the ceilings and the shelving units still screwed into place.

Killian toed his foot into dust, then glance up with a grin. "If you put a business in this place what would it be?"

It didn't take her more than two seconds to answer. "A restaurant. A decent one where people could be waited on by someone not in short shorts and served something other than burgers and fries."

"Ah, right, I can see that. I thought you might suggest a book store or a coffee bar."

Darcy tilted her head, considering the idea. "Specialty coffees, just coffee, with a pastry would be nice, too. What made you decide to go into business?"

"You."

"Me? How do you go from cop to businessman?"

"I became a cop out of respect to my father. It was never my dream."

"Is your dream running a restaurant?"

"It could be, especially with you. My main dream as goofy as it might sound to you is to live in a small town where everyone knows your name. I would eventually like to raise a family. Right now, I might need to find a business partner/girlfriend."

"Thinking you can get a two for one deal."

"I like to remain hopeful. What do you think?"

Instead of answering, she whirled and threw herself into his arms. Over Killian's shoulder, she could see Grandpa Willie and his two friends holding up signs that read SAY YES DARCY.

Of course, the town knew.

"You realize it will be a very public romance."

"It already is."

She kept one arm wrapped around Killian, but gave a thumbs up to her crowd of three who gave a cheer.

"What was that?"

"I think it was my fan club. There are a few things I might need to work out, though."

"Already dictating terms." Killian scrunched his nose. "Go on."

"The jewel thieves, what about them? How can I relax never knowing what might happen?"

He rested his forehead against hers. "No worries. The recently released felon, Boris Kaploff, was picked up in your former minister's home, trashing the place after breaking in."

"Former minister?"

"He and his wife hopped a plane to the Caribbean. One way tickets."

"Sounds suspicious. Will the police go after them?"

"Nope. There isn't enough evidence. However, I did pass on the information to an insurance investigator. You have nothing to worry about."

"I wouldn't go that far, but things are looking up. I'd be glad to help you with the restaurant, but I have two requirements."

"They are?"

"We have to hire Ruby."

"Is she any good at waitressing?"

"I have no clue, but at least she'd get Bruce McCormick to drop in for lunch every day. After him, others will follow."

He raised his head enough to drop a kiss on her hair. "Good plan. Should I ask what your other requirement is?"

Darcy leaned back to see his eyes. "I need to edit my suspense novel and want you to serve as my police expert."

"Can do. Should I ask what your plot line is?"

"It's all about a charismatic suspense writer who witnesses an actual crime, but can't get anyone to believe her."

"Is there a sexy Black Irish cop involved?"

"There could be."

"Would there be some hot scenes?"

"Guaranteed."

"I'll take the job, but you do understand a great deal of research will be needed."

"I was counting on it." Darcy rested her chin on Killian's shoulder and noticed the town watchmen had drifted away. Maybe she underestimated the townspeople. It was all a matter of perception. Now, that she realized the part they played in her rescue, Darcy had no regrets about not leaving, especially since the town's newest resident changed everything.

THE END

Ready for the third book in
The Men of Machismo Series?
Diagnosis: Trouble

JEWEL NODDED AT the handsome intern, unwilling to return his broad smile. Yeah, she knew who he was. The nurses' lounge buzzed like a busy hive with Declan Winters being the newest topic of conversation. News that the bearded doctor was single made more than one nurse smile. Not her, never her, she'd not be that stupid. Her fingers clenched around the tray of lab samples the ER asked her to ferry up to the phlebotomy unit.

Doctors were unavoidable in a hospital. Too bad, most of them considered themselves demi-gods or goddesses. Some of the male doctors tended to confuse the nurses with another profession. Only the threat of a sexual harassment suit kept them from backing the prettier nurses into the available supply closet. Her lips firmed as she considered the handsy physicians. It didn't matter if they were married or not. One of the senior doctors who could have served as a commercial model for thoughtful older physician with his graying hair and wrinkled countenance had the nerve to whisper in her ear that his wife didn't mind.

Forget the wife, she minded. Her loud refusal ended up with her demoted to working in the emergency room. The six months she worked weekends to escape the hellish assignment wiped out in a single swoop. Kelly, her best friend, urged her to report the physician. Too bad, she didn't. To say anything now would sound like carping and wouldn't solve anything.

Finally, she reached the tiny phlebotomy lab. Jackie, her friend, stood and reached for the tray.

"Appreciate you bringing the tray up. We're down a person today and had no one to fetch and carry. Surprised you could get away."

Her shoulders went up in a shrug, still reflecting on the cool reception she received from one nurse. "I had time. Sometimes, I'm just glad to escape, but apparently, it doesn't appear to be any better on any other floor. I'm still a pariah."

"Oh please." Jackie wrinkled her nose. "You're just fresh news."

"You know I got kicked back downstairs because I refused old garlic breath."

Her friend's lip twisted as she shook her head. "The fact you were so loud about it is what got you in trouble. Did you forget who was in the administrator's golfing foursome?"

Golfing foursomes didn't cross her mind as she had wrestled with the randy doctor to keep her smock top down and her dignity intact. "It would be good if they'd print this stuff and hand it out to beginning nurses. I'd go to another hospital if I thought I could get a good recommendation." It hadn't been the first time she considered such a drastic move.

"Wait, it will pass, especially with the new intern." Jackie's eyes rolled upward. "I can't remember his name.

"Declan Winters." She sighed unwillingly to listen to another woman gush about the man.

Her friend grinned at her and winked. "Not so unaffected as you like to pretend, huh?"

"Hell, the last thing I need is to get involved with a narcissistic doctor. I learned my lesson the hard way."

Romantic Comedy Fan?
Check out Steamy Interludes series

A sexy, younger man pursues Ashlee; she's almost decided to let him catch her.

The very last thing Ashlee expected was to meet a hot, younger guy Nick, at her boyfriend's funeral. The tall, soft-spoken man comforted her with stories of her boyfriend since he studied under him. Grateful for Nick's help and the mutual connection they both shared with the deceased, they kept in contact.

Ashlee managed to ignore his hints for drinks and meetings, putting it down to politeness. He felt sorry for her. There was no way he could be interested in a woman at least a decade older than he was. That was until her work posse caught scent of the story and urged her to give the man a chance. Ashlee knew she had to be the most reluctant cougar in the history of womankind, but what did she have to lose?

Deidre takes a walk on the uninhibited side.

What if all your life consisted of was, work and therapy dates where middle-aged men talked about their fears in a home cooking restaurant? Maybe it would even make you long for something new, even, a little wild. It did Deidre.

Call it an impulsive choice, but she finally caved into Curt, a police officer who just returned to duty after being wounded in a sting operation, who wasn't taking no for an answer. Going out with a cop, fourteen years her junior was irrational according to her friends. Meeting Curt for drinks was just the beginning. What she didn't expect was the flash fire that developed between them and the possibility it could burn out of control.

Can Theo outmaneuver her high school nemesis, a persistent ex-boyfriend, and a wayward pup to win the affections of the town's newest vet?

Theo discovers her husband and sister doing the mattress dance on her 1000 count sheets. She tosses the sheets, husband, and any future romantic aspirations, but holds on to her sister, begrudgingly.

A pint-sized devil dog propels romance-phobic Theo into Dr. Brent Knight's office and arms. Unfortunately, her old high school rival, a persistent ex-boyfriend who hasn't got his head around that they're not a couple, and her own heart serves as speed bumps on the way to love.

A mysterious man gives Darla the weekend of her life. (FREE)

Darla never had time for love. Even though she worked in the perfume industry that epitomizes romance. No appropriate male ever wandered into the picture. Maybe that's why she accepted her friend's suggestion to fix up her up. Desperation and a desire to make sure she even remembered how to act like a woman as opposed to a corporate warrior.

Too bad, her arranged date fell on the eve before her meeting with some hot shot Italian nobleman she needed to sign for her company's continued success. Even more ironic, her blind date Alex besides being the poster child for all things delicious had a sexy Italian accent. The accent alone should have reminded her of the need to prepare for her meeting. Instead charmed by his old world manners and animal magnetism she allows him to take charge and forgets about business. Two things she's never done before.

Cinda is a practical woman with a very impractical Christmas Desire.

Cinda isn't ready to become a glorious butterfly. She's still in the caterpillar stage with her generous curves. All she really wants is for a man to appreciate who she is. The way Jack did when they met at the airport. They shared a romantic day as they both waited for their flights. He kissed her goodbye and tucked his card in her suit pocket with instructions to call. It figures she'd lose his card. Luck never dealt her a romantic winning hand, but it's time to reshuffle the cards.

Six months fantasizing about Jack was enough. Raven determines not only to help her friend to become the butterfly she is, but also to give her friend a gift she'll never forget. Cinda voices her doubts about attending the masquerade ball. Raven reveals that Santa left her special gift at the ball. Her job is to retrieve it.

Marcus's name and appearance in her writing class is bogus, but his effect on Teresa is very real.

Dating's tough in small towns. The smart women gobbled up the town's eligible bachelors while Teresa obtained her degree out of state. Back home in Kentucky and teaching at the local high school, she finds herself competing for the attention of the taxidermist with a tricked out truck and a dentist who thinks he's the reincarnation of James Dean.

A sexy stranger appears in her adult education class. The man is definitely no townie with his exotic looks and even stranger accent. It's obvious he's lying about why he's in her class, but that doesn't dampen his appeal. There was a rule against staff and students fraternizing, but she might be tempted to break it.

Elise has to play dirty to win her man.

A divorced marriage counselor doesn't inspire confidence, which is the reason Elise dons a wedding ring. Her fake marriage status results in her slipping to the other side town to date. The man she sees the most is Jackson the bartender at the local seafood restaurant.

Her clients think he's her husband. Unfortunately, someone else has her eye on the handsome bartender.

Author Notes

Some of you may have noticed that book two wasn't **Diagnosis Trouble.** Darcy and Killian's story would not wait. It's a good thing in a way because I have an entirely new twist for the **Diagnosis Trouble**, a deadly one.

- If you enjoyed this book, please lend it to a friend.
- Write a review.
- Do you have an idea for a story or a character name? Love to hear it. I can be reached through my website at www.morgankwyatt.com
- Want to get free books, read excerpts before everyone else, receive special members only swag and giveaways? You need to be on the mailing list. Go over to my website and sign up. (I don't sell my mailing list and guard it as well as I do my chocolate.)
- Do you like humor with your mystery? Check out my new cozy mystery series that I wrote with my husband. Book one of *The Painted Lady Inn Mysteries* is **Murder Mansion**. We write under the combined name of M.K. Scott.
- Check out the Morgan K Wyatt books too. **He Loves Me Not,** romantic suspense.
- Love to meet you, check out my personal appearances on the website too.
- Can you do one more thing? Go out and have an amazing day.

Morgan Kay